The Gift of Christmas Yet to Come

A St Nicholas Bay novella

Jo Bartlett

Copyright © 2014 Fabrian Books.

All rights reserved. This book or any portion thereof may not be reproduced or used in any manner without the express written permission of the publisher, except for the use of brief quotations in a book review.

Typesetting and Design Fabrian Books – fabrianbooks.com.

Copy Editing Tessa Shapcott.

Jo Bartlett asserts the right to be identified as the author of this book. All the characters and events in this book are fictional. Any resemblance to individuals is purely unintentional.

For my husband and children -

the only people with whom I want to spend every Christmas yet to come.

And for my Mum, who's still a proud parent, even of a daughter my age!

With grateful thanks to all my family and friends for their patience and support, especially my wonderful writing family – The Write Romantics.

Special thanks to my gang of beta readers for this novella, who have been so generous with their time – Paula, Julie, Lynne, Jennie and Steve.

Thanks too to Tessa Shapcott for her input with the line editing - an editor who was a real pleasure to work with.

How It All Began

I was never the sort of person who believed in fortune tellers, fate mapping out my life or messages from beyond the grave. At least not until I encountered a woman who changed all that.

Contrary to popular belief, and the confession above, teachers are normal human beings. Most of them, anyway. There are a couple of my colleagues I wouldn't like to vouch for. But, in the main, we're pretty average, with the same hopes and fears as other people—and a phobia of school inspectors, of course.

Back when I was in high school, and the seeds of all this were sown, I was convinced that teachers came from a different planet, or were plugged into the mains at night with the rest of the equipment, only switched on when the caretaker came to open up in the mornings. They were so serious and straight-laced, always worrying about homework, or whether I'd signed up for any activities that might look good on my university application. They didn't have real lives, real problems, and I was certainly *never* going to be one.

I can still remember the shock, aged fifteen, when I'd snuck into a nightclub with fake ID and enough hairspray to weld a car roof on and I'd seen the head of history—dancing. I couldn't take my eyes off him. Not because I liked him, he was ancient after all—he must have been all of thirty at the time—or because he was a particularly bad dancer; in fact, he looked more or less like everyone else. That *was* the shock, I suppose, the reason I was so transfixed. He wasn't beamed up to the mother ship when the final school bell rang, or plugged in with the rest of the robots; he was out, with friends—real, non-teacher types—laughing and looking for all the world like he knew how to have *fun*.

Despite this one exception, the rest of the staff steadfastly upheld my belief that they only existed between the hours of nine and three-thirty, and were dedicated to sucking as much fun out of my life during those six and a half hours as possible. Miss Bone, who taught Latin, was among the worst of them. She singled out three of us from my class for extra tuition; not because we had potential, or because we were falling behind but, as it had seemed back then, simply to torture us. If you'd told me she was going to change the course of my life, I'd have laughed until my face hurt. Only Miss Bone had a secret—one we wouldn't truly discover until much later, when we'd finally left the confines of St Nicholas Bay High—and she'd chosen us for a reason.

Chapter One

I'd always loved the run-up to Christmas at school. It was the perfect excuse to get out the glitter-glue and go back to a time when all I was worried about was whether I'd been good enough for Santa Claus to finally deliver that Barbie townhouse I'd had my eye on for the past six months. Looking around the classroom on the last day of term, I allowed myself a moment of quiet satisfaction, the sort you can only get at the end of the day, when the last of the children has been married up with their belongings and despatched to the parent patiently waiting to collect them. They'd surpassed themselves; Christmas Decoration Day had seen new highs in creativity. There were unicorn-reindeer hybrids, a dolphin in a Christmas hat sitting on a deckchair and even the three Wise Men, all with purple skin. It was my second Christmas as Special Needs Coordinator at St Nicholas Bay Juniors and my tenth as class teacher—that last bit was difficult to believe.

'Ready, Kate?' Sara Walton had pushed opened the door to my classroom and removed her black-rimmed glasses, massaging the point where they'd pinched her nose. They weren't prescription lenses, just clear glass, but they were her "Clark Kent" disguise, as she put it; a force field to make her authoritative and ward off parents who tried to overstep the mark. Having seen her in action as the school's office manager, I knew she could be tough, and not even Superman could make her back down once she'd made up her mind. Take the glasses off and she was still my Sara, though; best friends since those days at high school and Miss Bone's extra

Latin lessons. I never dreamt back then that I'd become a teacher—it would have seemed like a fate worse than death—or that we'd end up working together, and with Will, another boy from our year. But St Nicholas Bay had that effect on people; it drew you in and never really let you go.

'I'm as ready as I'll ever be.' Straightening-up the quiz papers that would have to wait to be marked, I smiled. It was the staff Christmas meal at the Mexican restaurant just up from the harbour. We always went out straight from school—the annual get-together tended to be a long session—and this year the head teacher had promised the first round was on her.

'Great! Have you got your Secret Santa?' She patted the package under her arm, and I scooped up the present I'd bought from under my desk. Just my luck to pick Gary's name from the hat—an IT technician with a passion for *Lord of the Rings*, who may as well have been speaking in Elvish half the time. Thank goodness for the Internet; I just had to hope he didn't already own a Gollum night-light.

St Nicholas Bay's steep high street led down from the primary and high schools, which faced each other at the top of the hill, to the small harbour that gave the town part of its name. Christmas was always the biggest event in the town's calendar, and the aroma of gingerbread and cinnamon filled the air as Sara and I made our way down to Nachos At The Bay.

'Feels a bit disloyal, not going the traditional route and having a proper Dickens-style Christmas do, doesn't it?' Sara laughed. 'Shouldn't we be out looking for the biggest turkey in the shop window?'

'I think as paupers we'd be stuffing an anorexic goose like Bob Cratchit, but I'm sure they're doing it properly in Fezziwig's.' I gestured towards the sixteenth-century coaching inn on the other side of the road. Its heavily-latticed casement windows were steeped in what looked like artificial snow-spray. If the legend was true, and Charles Dickens really had penned some of *A Christmas Carol* there, he'd surely be turning in his grave.

At some point in its history, the town had taken the legend and run with it. Everywhere from Tiny Tim's Toys, run by our old school friend, Meg Andrews, to Marley's Chains, the family-run hardware store, got in on the act. Growing up in a town that traded on a link to Christmas all year round, and was named after Santa Claus himself, had been a great way to spend your childhood. Maybe that's why locals who left, like Will and I, had found our way back here, years after leaving, and reformed the friendships with those who'd stayed behind as strongly as though we'd never left.

'No, they can keep their tradition, I'm looking forward to turkey burritos,' Sara winked, her blonde fringe flopping over her eyes with the exaggerated effort, 'and to the opening of the Secret Santa surprises, of course.'

'You haven't, have you?' I shivered, walking under one of the sets of lights, strung all across the high street, depicting scenes from Dickens' novel. The Ghost of Christmas Yet to Come was just up ahead—I'd always hated that one.

'Haven't what?' Sara widened her baby-blue eyes, and I knew she was guilty.

'Wangled it, so you got to be my Secret Santa again and could buy something even worse than last time.' I winced as we walked under the Ghost of Christmas Yet to Come. 'Although quite how you could beat handing me a blow-up man to unwrap, as I'm sitting next to the Chair of Governors, I'm not quite sure.'

The shop window of Nachos At the Bay, one of the few places not to cash in on the Dickens effect, was decorated with strings of Christmas lights in golds, greens and reds. Inside, there were more lights but, instead of a tree, almost all of the surfaces, and every table, had a large red poinsettia placed upon it. There was an over-sized nativity scene on one of the two dressers that flanked either side of a traditional stucco fireplace, and a similar scene with characters from *A Christmas Carol* on the other.

As we walked in, Will looked up and gestured to the two empty seats next to him. Thank God our deputy head wasn't just a pretty face; he'd done as asked and saved us a spot as far away from the Chair of Governors as possible.

'I can't believe you managed it.' Grinning, I sat down next to him, taking off my coat and hat and hoping the latter hadn't left me with a severe case of helmet hair. 'I felt sure that Immy would be welded to your side by now.' I laughed and he managed a wry smile. It was difficult to get away from your stalker when she worked in the same building as you. Ever since Imogen Rogers had started as the reception class teacher, the Easter before, she'd followed Will around like a lost puppy.

'It took some doing, I can tell you.' Will's green eyes flickered as Immy shot a venomous look at us from the other end of the table, and he lowered his voice. 'I keep telling her it's school policy that staff can't have relationships, but it doesn't seem to make any difference.'

'You'll have to get some contact lenses for work. You know how sexy she finds those glasses you only wear when you're marking and the way you stick your tongue out when you're really concentrating. In fact we all do; she's said it often enough!' I moved my hand, just in time to stop Will stabbing it with a fork. If we turned into a couple of eight-year-olds sometimes, I wouldn't change it for the world.

'Why don't you just tell her you don't fancy her?' Sara leant across me and I thought for a moment she might don her "Clark Kents" to make the point more forcefully. 'Honesty is always better in the long run.'

'That's easy for you to say. It's not you who keeps finding love notes and cookies with our initials on, cut into the shape of love hearts.' Will ran a hand through his dark hair.

'Is that what those biscuits on your desk were supposed to be? It looked more like a uterus than a heart to me.' Sara glanced in my direction and dropped another of her none-too-subtle winks. 'Still, could be. Tick-tock, tick-tock and all that, eh, Kate?'

Two hours later, I had eaten so much that the waistband of my trousers was making an angry red mark on the skin beneath it, and I'd also drunk far more wine than I'd been planning to. It was at this point that Sara stood up and clapped her hands together—it was coming, whether I wanted it to or not: Secret Santa time.

'Okay, everyone, it's that moment you've all been waiting for.' She looked around the table at us, as though she actually believed what she was saying. 'Time to exchange gifts. But, so no-one knows who was whose Secret Santa, if you just pile them all at the top of the table I can hand them out.'

If there'd been any doubt who'd been responsible for buying my present, it was quashed the moment I opened it. Okay, so it wasn't as overtly embarrassing as the inflatable man, but it might as well have been for all the colour that washed across my face.

'That looks professional.' Will picked up the stainless steel turkey baster I'd just unwrapped and raised an eyebrow. We both knew my cooking skills didn't extend much beyond a cuppa soup.

'It looks almost medical to me.' Fiona Bright, our headmistress, who could eavesdrop in the way that only really experienced teachers can, joined the conversation. This was all I needed, an inquisition about exactly why I might want a turkey baster with an injector attachment. So I mumbled something about wanting to keep the meat moist, whilst Sara dissolved into hysterics, just to the right of me. Still, it wasn't all bad; at least Gary didn't already own a Gollum night-light and I wasn't sure I'd ever seen him looking so happy.

'Remind me to kill you, next time we're alone together, so there's no chance of a witness.' I toyed briefly with storming off into the night and leaving Sara to explain to Will why I was in such a strop over the turkey baster, but I couldn't trust her not to make things sound worse than they really were. I knew not everyone was going to accept my decision, but I'd rather tell them in my own way, without the Jeremy Kyle-style slant Sara would inevitably put on it.

'No one else knew why I'd bought it.' She was giggling again. 'They just think you've come over all Gordon Ramsay, or more likely that I just bought the first vaguely Christmas related thing I saw. T'is the season to baste your turkey, after all.'

'Is someone going to tell me what's actually going on?' Will caught hold of my arm, my long, dark hair swinging like a curtain as I turned to look at him.

'What's going on is that I made the mistake of telling my ex-best friend here that I was thinking of taking steps to get pregnant.'

'I didn't realise you were even seeing someone.' Will still had hold of my arm and he clearly hadn't quite put two and two together.

'She isn't, you wally, that's the whole point.' Sara widened her eyes to hammer home the point.

'Oh, I see.' Will looked at me for a long moment, but I wasn't entirely sure he did.

Chapter Two

The Old St Nickers was a name that only Sara could have been responsible for. We officially ran the alumni events for St Nicholas Bay High, but had come together as a result of Miss Bone singling us out, years before. There were the three of us from my old class: Sara, me and Meg; then there was Will from the other form in our year, and six more ex-pupils from the two years below us. We'd all been Miss Bone's protégées in her final years at the school, when she'd discovered her *gift* and let us into the secret. Of course Sara and I had laughed at first, called the old girl mad—with her thick American-tan tights and the leg hair that poked through—what could someone like her tell *us* about life? But Meg had always believed it, long before I'd admitted that Miss Bone's gift was real and had come to rely on her advice for anything that really mattered.

It was funny how we'd all ended up back in the Bay, "the chosen ones", as Joan had called us. Sara and I had laughed for hours about that too, when we'd first heard her Christian name. Joan Bone; her parents must have had a sense of humour, or perhaps they were very cruel—although we never found out. Miss Bone never said anything about herself—past, present or future—she only wanted to talk about us.

'I can read yellow auras.' She'd just blurted it out in the middle of our second extra-curricular Latin lesson. I'd looked from Sara to Meg and back again, wondering if it was some kind of Latin textbook I was supposed to have heard of.

'Whadya mean, Miss?' Sara, who I recall had bright pink hair at the time, looked just as confused as I was.

'All three of you girls have yellow auras. It means you're spiritual, and it also means I can be your guide, tell you the right path to take. They're the only auras I can read.' Miss Bone had looked over her half-moon spectacles, as if daring us to object. None of us spoke. I wanted to, but I could feel the laughter bubbling in my throat. If I'd opened my mouth, that would have been it. 'You've got some big decisions coming up, applications for university and such like, and I was hoping you'd let me help you.'

'I'm not sure I want to go at all, Miss.' It was Meg who'd spoken up first, giving Miss Bone that earnest look she wore so well. She was top of the class because of it—of course she'd be going to university.

Miss Bone closed her eyes and seconds later they shot open again. 'I can see your path, Megan. It's here, in the Bay, with children, but you won't be a teacher. You'll be in a business of your own that brings everyone who uses your services joy.' Miss Bone sat down for a moment, as if aura-reading was an exhausting pastime rather than a big heap of nonsense.

'What about me, Miss?' Sara stood up and began sashaying up and down the classroom, her hands on her hips. She was going to be a model, we all knew that; she'd told us often enough.

'You'll be a mum before you think you're ready, but it will be the right thing, so don't let it pass you by and miss your chance.' Miss Bone gave Sara such a serious look that she said nothing. It was like having some weird dream, the sort I got if I ate too much cheese, only Miss Bone was looking at me and taking in a long breath.

'You'll be the one to go to university, Kate, but it shouldn't be for art; you should be a teacher.' There was no doubt in her voice, but she had to be joking, didn't she? Me? Teach? No way on earth was I going to end up in a dead-end job like that. I told the girls as much as soon as we were out of the classroom. Sara had laughed it off too. We were barely seventeen, and there was no chance of her having a baby before she'd graced the cover of Vogue.

She was pregnant by the following Christmas. It was just a coincidence of course, Sara being feckless as usual. At least that's what I'd told myself. I don't know whether Miss Bone's words stayed with her, but she decided to keep the babies—twins as it turned out—and she and Joe got married a year later, on her eighteenth birthday. When the twins were three, doctors found a tumour during a routine check-up and Sara ended up having a hysterectomy just shy of her twenty-first birthday. They'd been dark days and I wasn't around to support her, because I was at uni. But she'd got through it with Joe and the twins, and here they were, nearly sixteen years on, still a happy little family unit.

Miss Bone, one; logical explanation, nil.

Meg started work in the toy shop in town straight out of school and bought the lease with her husband, James, just after they got married ten years later. They added their son, Riley, to the family three years after that. Tiny Tim's Toys was every bit the draw for children, young and old, that Miss Bone had predicted it would be.

Lucky guesses and coincidence? Back in those extra Latin lessons I thought so too. I'd made up my mind to study art and that was it. I wanted to be a sculptor, but then I did some work experience in my final year and everything changed. I had a placement at a school for the blind for six weeks, helping out in the pottery and sculpture classes, and I fell in love—with teaching, and with the children, whose special needs often extended far beyond their visual impairment. I'd found my vocation, my *raison d'etre*, but Miss Bone had known it all along.

So here we were, knocking on the door of our mid-thirties, all back together in the Bay and still just as ready to ask Miss Bone's advice. She'd retired three years after we'd left school, which was why there were only the ten of us in the Old St Nickers "secret" group, but she must have helped hundreds of others since. We were her first though, and all the more special because of it; at least that's what she always told us.

Chapter Three

It was four days before Christmas and we were in Will's cottage, waiting for the other six from the years below to join us for an Old St Nickers Christmas drink. Apparently, we were also about to discuss my inner most secrets—whether I liked it or not.

'So you're still thinking about it, Kate, the sperm donor thing?' Meg was sitting cross-legged on Will's floor and giving me that earnest look she'd never lost. 'I think you're rushing into it, and I've been thinking you should watch this.' She thrust a DVD into my hand and I turned it over carefully. I wasn't sure what I was expecting, but it wasn't that.

'*The Back-Up Plan*?'

'Yes, have you seen it?' Meg's eyebrows knitted together above her brown eyes as she spoke. 'It's the one where Jennifer Lopez gets pregnant from a sperm donation and finally meets the man of her dreams *the same day*.' She really emphasised that last part. 'That could happen to you!'

'Yes, because my life's a Hollywood movie. Look at me; term finished a week ago and I'm still picking the glitter out of my hair.'

'I just can't see what the rush is, that's all.' Meg shrugged, and I knew I'd upset her. It was the last thing I wanted but I had to make them all—my closest friends—understand. This was my decision and something that had been on my mind for a very long time.

'I've been thinking about it for a while, but it's that coming-to-the-end-of-another-year thing.' I tried to make lighter of it than I felt. 'Next year is the year I need to make it happen. I have to get pregnant by the time I'm thirty-five or my chances are going to drop like a stone. I've read all the statistics and they're not pretty.'

'Could you freeze your eggs?' Will spoke for the first time, and I shook my head.

'There's a risk they won't thaw properly and, anyway, I don't want to start the whole thing in my forties, I want a child while I've still got the energy to bring him or her up and work at the same time.' I swallowed the lump in my throat; it was much harder to talk about than I'd thought. 'I love my job and I don't want to give it up, but I want it all—a child, a career—and, you know what, the thing I'm least worried about is having a man. I've got my family and you guys, and that's all I need.'

'You should do it. Just look at me, if I hadn't had the twins when I did, that would have been it.' Sara grabbed Will's iPad off the side and started tapping on the screen.

'It's got a password: my date of birth...'

'Yep, guessed that and already put it in.' Sara grinned at him. 'I hack into your computer at work all the time too. Now let's see... okay, *sperm donation cost*.'

'It's eight hundred and fifty pounds for the donation.' I managed a rueful smile, as Will caught my eye. Okay, so I'd memorised the price, but so would he if he'd been on the website as often as I had. 'Then another twelve hundred-ish for the technical bit, or almost treble the price if I need IVF.'

'We're obviously in the wrong business, and it makes my £12 turkey baster look even more of a bargain.' Sara laughed. 'Seriously, though, isn't there anyone you could ask to do it more... old school?'

For a moment all eyes turned to Will, but I quickly shook my head again. The last thing I wanted was that kind of complication.

'No, if I'm going to do it, it's going to be this way. Then I can pick out someone who's got hazel eyes like me and maybe the baby will get them too. I can decide to stick in some tall-people genes, like you two inherited.' I gestured towards Will and Meg. 'I can even pick a nuclear physicist with a PhD, if I want to have conversation with my child that I don't understand by the time they're five.' I slid the DVD into my bag and silently prayed one of the others would show up, so we could stop the critique of my lifestyle choices. People got pregnant after a one-night stand all the time and no-one batted an eyelid. So why was planning it carefully—and safely—so shocking?

'At least promise me you'll speak to Miss Bone before you do anything drastic?' Meg twisted a strand of her red hair around her finger, and all I could do was nod. Speaking to Miss Bone was a given, anyway. I knew she'd support me on this, she had to.

'Do you think we can ring Childline, claim to have been left home alone at Christmas... in our mid-thirties?' Will was pouring us another glass of wine, as I ladled juices over the turkey which was far too big for the two of us, as if I knew what I was doing. We'd be eating turkey sandwiches, turkey curry and turkey cobbler until well into the New Year at this rate. 'I could always sing you a song if you get scared without your mum and dad?' Will winked.

I'd never forgotten our first day at school, when I'd been four years old and scared stiff, as our mums pushed us gently but firmly into the reception class. I'd clutched Will's hand like my life depended on it, and a big, fat tear had rolled down my face and plopped on to my new patent shoes. Will had looked at me and started to sing a song called *Blackbird*, the same one our mums had sung to us at the playgroup we'd gone to until we'd started school. I'd felt better immediately and, ever since then, it had been our little joke. Will had sung it to me when I'd been waiting to have my tonsils out aged twelve, and whenever I'd needed a laugh, after break-ups and disastrous job interviews, and it always did the trick. Once his voice had broken, his ability to sing had broken with it, so mostly he just hummed it instead. But if I *really* needed cheering up, he'd sing it for me, and there was no chance of keeping a straight face with that sound echoing in my ears.

'I think I'm okay for now, but I am *not* in my mid-thirties. Thirty-three and three-quarters still qualifies as early thirties in my book.' I grinned at him. 'But I do think our parents going off on a cruise together and leaving us to cook our own Christmas dinner was some sort of deliberate message that we need to get our personal lives in order.' It wasn't quite as desperate as it sounded, as neither of us was still living at home. Will's cottage just off the harbourside had a glorious sea view, and I had a nice flat, with two bedrooms and a tiny box-room of a study, five minutes' walk from the high street. But we lived in the same town as our parents, who themselves had been neighbours and best friends since before we were born, so we hadn't entirely cut those apron strings. Will had tried, once, not dashing straight back after university like me, but St Nicholas Bay had drawn him home again—at some considerable cost.

'How do they feel about the whole donation thing?' Will passed me a glass. It was funny how people avoided mentioning the "S" word, as though they could just about cope with it if they steered clear of that.

'I don't think Mum cares how I get pregnant, she's just desperate for a grandchild now she's retired and there's only me to fulfil that.' I shrugged. Perhaps there was some pressure from elsewhere, but I wanted a child, a family of my own, more than anything. It had started as a niggle when I'd turned thirty, and almost four years later it had become an ache. There'd been boyfriends, don't get me wrong, but they'd all turned out, somehow or another, to be a worse prospect than the thought of going it alone.

'And your dad?' This time Will widened his eyes and I suppressed the urge to laugh. He knew as well as I did how old-fashioned my father was, and Dad had gone as white a sheet when I'd first broached the idea. He'd accepted it though, preferring not to think of the mechanics at all, just focusing on the end result. As traditional as he was, I knew he loved me unconditionally and, in the end, that was all that mattered. However a child came about, he'd love them that way too.

'He's okay about it now, but you know Dad, he took some time to come to terms with it.' I took a sip of wine and looked at Will. 'How about you? Do you get the *when-are-we-going-to-be-grandparents* question? I know you've got all the time in the world, what with being a man.'

'No, they don't really say much at all about that sort of thing. I think they're still treading on eggshells about the whole Louisa situation. They blame themselves partly for me coming home, but it wasn't just that.' Will lowered his gaze. It was clearly still a tough time of year, three years and three months since he'd come home to start the new school year as Deputy Head of St Nicholas Bay Juniors, and almost three years to the day since his wife, Louisa, had decided she didn't like life in the Bay.

'I thought it was the job you came for. Although I suppose there are plenty of deputy heads' jobs in Wales too. So your parents must have been part of the draw?'

'Them, and old friends.' Will caught my eye for a second. 'But you know, Louisa never really took to the old crowd.' That was an understatement. We'd first met her when they were at university together in Wales and we'd gone up there for a weekend of partying. Even a heavily pregnant Sara had made the trip, but Louisa had been frosty. Her home town was only ten miles from the university, so she'd left after half a day in our company to catch up with *her* old friends, as she put it. Clearly she didn't want to make new friends out of us.

Will had got his first teaching job up there, after he'd finished his degree. They'd bought a house together and five years later they'd tied the knot. We all went, of course, and Sara's twins were even bridesmaid and page boy, but it was all under duress, as far as Louisa was concerned, and you'd have to be pretty thick-skinned not to pick up on it. That's why we'd all been so surprised when Will had taken the job back in the Bay, so close to the bottom south east corner of England that we were literally in danger of falling into the sea. We'd been much less surprised when Louisa had hot-footed it home for Christmas, less than three months later, and never come back.

'Yes, she always made it pretty clear she thought we were a bad influence on you. And as for our trust in Miss Bone, I think that drove her almost potty!' I laughed and for a moment I was sorry for Louisa; it must have been hard, how close we all were and for so long.

'She blamed Miss Bone more than all of you.' Will closed his eyes briefly. 'Said it was her claptrap that had swayed my decision to take the job back here.'

'And was it?'

'I suppose a little bit. She told me years before the offer came up, when I came back to visit my parents, that my aura would never be settled until I came home.' Will sighed. 'I was looking for answers when the job came up and it all seemed to fit. I missed the old crowd, things with Louisa were already difficult and I suppose I did use Miss Bone's words from years earlier as a deciding factor. I forgot to think about what made Louisa happy though.'

'Do you regret it?' I watched as an expression I couldn't quite pin down crossed Will's face.

'No. I *am* happier here, and I've come to realise that whatever it is that makes Louisa happy, it isn't me. So, in the long term, it wouldn't have mattered whether we'd stayed in Wales together or here. It just wasn't meant to be.'

'So Miss Bone was spot-on once again.' I felt a frisson of nerves as I spoke, suddenly worried that she might warn me off my plans for starting a family. Would I listen if she did?

'It seems so.' Will looked at me for a long moment. 'Look if you're determined to do this donation thing and if Miss Bone sees it as the right path, will you let me help you?'

'I…' What could I say? Will was wonderful, but I didn't want the complication of a dad being around who wasn't part of a partnership with me.

'It's alright, I could tell by your face when everyone looked at me the other night that you wouldn't have wanted me to volunteer for the *really* important job.' He gave me a half-smile. 'But if you need a male role model, or someone to help you out with the practical stuff—you know, helping you to decorate, baby-sitting when you need a break, and all that—I hope you know I'm your man.'

'If only I'd met someone like you, Will, I wouldn't need all this.' I squeezed his hand. It was what I loved about St Nicholas Bay, the friendships so long standing that we didn't need explanations. Will would make a great dad when the time came, and I'd be there for him too, if he needed me. Whatever Miss Bone thought she could see in my aura, I knew I could cope with being a single mum because I'd never really be alone in St Nicholas Bay.

Chapter Four

as iron – it was a line from that
ristmas carols and somehow
he occasion, gathered as we were
Miss Bone. The grass was white
touches of frost glittering in the
winter sunlight far too weak to see it off. The grave had been carved from frozen earth by a mechanical digger brought in for the job. It was as though the ground had been as unwilling to accept Miss Bone as we were to let her go. January, never my favourite time of year, was now forever tied up with losing the teacher and guide we'd taken for granted for more than fifteen years. Worse than that, I'd never got to ask her the really critical question—probably the single most important decision of my life—and now I'd have to make it without her.

'I only spoke to her on Christmas day.' I hissed out of the side of my mouth to Meg, who was standing, pale faced, beside me. Will and Sara were on my other side, and on the opposite side of the grave the other six members of the Old St Nickers committee stood in a sombre line. All of us had been affected by Miss Bone's guidance in some way, and the expressions on the faces of the other mourners suggested we weren't the only ones.

'Did you ask her then, you know, about your decision?' Meg whispered, turning towards me. I knew *she* didn't want me to do it, and that her argument against it had almost certainly been influenced by her own childhood.

'I doubt it would have been any good if I had. You know how she always needed to *see* our auras, to give us any guidance. But now I wish I'd asked, just to know what she thought of the idea in principle, whether she could see the outcome or not.'

We stopped talking as the vicar began to speak. I wish I could say that his words were a comfort, but he didn't know the real Miss Bone. He'd probably think her reading our auras to predict the future was, at best, nonsense and, at worst, the work of some sinister force. But even if it had all been in her mind, she'd been wise in a way you couldn't quite quantify and she'd changed our lives as a result. Only he *didn't* know that and so he spoke about her in a way that was unfamiliar to those of us who'd known the real Joan Bone. Finally, as the coffin was lowered into the ground and Will closed his hand around mine, softly humming the tune to *Blackbird*, I felt some comfort.

'Makes you realise how short life actually is, doesn't it?' As we walked away from the graveside, Sara wore one of her rare serious expressions. 'I don't think you should wait for a right moment that might never come, Kate. If having a family matters that much to you, then make it happen and make it now.'

'I think the cold air's got to her!' Will placed a hand on her forehead, a look of mock concern on his face. He was the one person I couldn't read when it came to all of this. Sara obviously thought I should go for it. Meg had serious doubts, but then she always did things by the book—life didn't work out that way for everyone.

I hadn't told the rest of the Old St Nickers my plans for parenthood; they were friends, but not in the way the original four of us from the same year at school were. The other girls were really close with one another, and if I'd mentioned it to one of them, then the rest would have known within seconds. Two of them, Rosie and Jas, had shops in the Bay, like Meg, and it might have been all over town by teatime if they'd known. It wouldn't have been malicious, but gossip was the life blood of the Bay and that would have fuelled it for weeks. I just didn't want to share the information yet, partly because it was so personal, but mainly in case it didn't work out. Living in St Nicholas Bay could be like a goldfish bowl at the best of times, so having people ask you every five minutes if you were pregnant would make it a lot worse. The two boys from the years below, well, men now, given that they were over thirty I suppose, weren't close friends of mine. Apart from Will, I'd always been a girl's girl when it came to friendships. Will had just always been there, next door or hanging out in the playground at school, and so we'd never had that awkwardness around each other, never had that boy-meets-girl tension.

'Well, since Sara's come over all serious, maybe we should get her out of the cold air.' I pulled the belt of my coat tighter, thinking about Miss Bone and what she'd done for us. Yet, in the end, she'd been alone. There was no close family to organise a wake but, in typical Joan style, she'd set the money aside to pay for the funeral itself. We'd celebrate her life, though, have a little party to give her the send-off she deserved. 'How about lunch at Belle's and a sherry or two in Joan's honour?'

'I'm up for lunch,' Sara grinned, 'but sod the sherry. I'm numb from the ankles down and the buttocks up, and only a treble brandy stands any chance of thawing me out.'

The owners of Belle's, happy to cash in on the Dickens connection and name their pub after Scrooge's lost love, eschewed the idea of a Victorian Christmas in every other respect. Whilst Fezziwig's looked like a Hollywood version of *A Christmas Carol* inside, spray-on snow excepted, Belle's looked like an explosion in Santa's Grotto. It was three days until Twelfth Night, so tinsel still hung in strands across the wall and there were giant baubles suspended from the ceiling that Will had to duck to avoid.

'So what's the one question you wished you'd asked Miss Bone before she died, then?' Sara swirled the brandy around her glass as she spoke, and we unashamedly hogged the warmth of the roaring log fire beside us. I was starting to feel my feet again, but their coming back to life wasn't an altogether comfortable sensation.

'I think you all know mine, so why don't *you* start, Sara?' Her expression changed at my words. There was definitely something on her mind.

'I would have asked her if she thought I should leave my job at the school and go to university.' Sara didn't make eye contact and there was a hint of colour in her cheeks that had nothing to do with her position next to the fire.

'But that's great, of course she'd want you to!' It was the best news I'd heard for a long time. There'd always been so much more to Sara than she gave herself credit for and she was finally seeing what the rest of us did. 'What are you planning to study?'

'I'm thinking nursing or midwifery, but it's all just an idea at the moment and I'm not sure how well it would go down at home.'

'You could deliver Kate's baby.' Meg shot me a look as she spoke and I couldn't help laughing.

'It takes years to qualify or even to be allowed to start helping out with stuff like that.' Sara frowned. She was much more serious about this than she was letting on. It had definitely gone beyond a vague idea.

'Exactly. It would be all the more reason for Kate to wait.' Meg crossed her arms, as if the decision were already made.

'She could wait too long, miss her chance.' Will looked wistful, as though he wasn't just talking about me.

'What about you, Will, what would you have asked?' Sara took the words out of my mouth and, for a moment, he was silent.

'Whether I'm destined to be alone.' He looked down at his pint and, not for the first time, I wanted to shake Louisa by the scruff of her neck. How she could have let someone like Will go was beyond me.

'Of course you won't!' I waited until he finally looked up. 'Half the female staff at the school are in love with you for a start.' He mumbled something that I didn't catch, but I didn't want to press him into talking about Louisa again. 'The only person keeping you single is you. Look at how Imogen Rogers was throwing herself at you at the Christmas do!'

'Don't remind me!' Will managed a grin. 'But even if she wasn't a nightmare, you know as well as

I do that relationships with colleagues are banned at the school.'

'I've never really understood why.' Sara took a large sip of her brandy and grimaced slightly. 'Mind you, there's never been anyone there who'd make me want to break the rule, even if I had been single. Will's like a brother, seventy per cent of the staff are female and the other blokes have hobbies ranging from *World of Warcraft* all-nighters to taxidermy. Then there's the lovely Gary, of course, and his *Lord of the Rings* obsession.'

'Just as well, given the Governors' stance on it. They think bringing the ups and downs of a relationship into the workplace is likely to have an impact on professionalism.' Will sounded like he was quoting from the staff handbook. 'And since I spend the rest of my time hanging out with you lot, I suppose I just got to wondering if I'm going to end up like Miss Bone.'

'You could always get Gary from IT to take you out on the pull with him!' Even as she said it, Sara was laughing. *The Lord of the Rings* conventions weren't known for their high female-to-male ratio.

'How about online dating?' Meg, ever practical, always wanting to sort everyone else's lives out for them, came up with the obvious solution.

'Well, I wouldn't rule it out, but I would have liked to ask Miss Bone if she saw something else in store for me.' Will clearly wasn't quite ready to be strong-armed into signing up for a three-month subscription to loveonline.com. 'What about you, Meg, what would you have asked?' He turned the question on her before she could press him any further.

'I would have asked her if I'll ever stop being afraid that what I've got might disappear. I've got everything I wanted, with James, the shop and Riley. But it's scary in a way, because I've got so much to lose.' Meg's eyebrows did their trick of knitting together again and then she relaxed. 'I know it's stupid, but if Miss Bone had told me she saw my life carrying on as it is for years, it would have been the answer I really wanted.'

'What you need, Meg, is something real to worry about.' Sara grinned, but it was good-natured teasing. Meg had always been a worrier and probably always would be. It was understandable, given what her mum had been through. 'So let's work out what the hell Kate should do, now we haven't got Miss Bone to ask for advice.'

'Actually, I've already been thinking about that.' Meg bent down to get something out of her bag and I wondered what was coming next. 'How about we go to this next month?' She handed me a small yellow leaflet.

'A spiritualist evening?' As I said the words, Sara nearly spat her brandy on to the table.

'I know what you're all thinking.' Meg shrugged. 'But we thought that about Miss Bone at first. Nan goes to spiritualist meetings all the time, and last time she went the medium put her in touch with one of her lost loved ones.'

'Was it your dad or your grandad?' Will asked the obvious question.

'Not exactly.' Meg shifted in her seat, as though she were trying to avoid the question. 'Alright, it was her dog, Teddy.'

'Your nan spoke to her dead dog?' Sara had a brilliantly dismissive look, that came quite naturally, but which she'd perfected over the years.

'She wanted to ask him why he'd jumped off the balcony.'

'Your nan's dog committed suicide?' I pressed my lips together to stem the hysteria that was threateningly close.

'If you'd tasted my Nan's cooking you'd understand!' Luckily Meg was grinning too. 'Okay, so it sounds ridiculous, but what if he really could get through to Miss Bone, get the answer to our questions?'

'And it would be a night out.' Sara grabbed the leaflet off me. 'Valentine's night? Suits me. Joe always forgets anyway, so it would stop me spending the night wanting to stab him for being so unromantic.'

'And we've established that I'm terminally single, so I'm up for it.' Will looked at me; they were all waiting for an answer.

'Alright, why not? I've got to start on a post-Christmas health kick before I do anything about getting pregnant, so one more month or so isn't going to make a difference.'

'It's a date then!' Meg raised her glass. 'To a new year of *endless* possibilities.'

I clinked my glass against hers and wondered what on earth I was letting myself in for.

Chapter Five

The first term after Christmas had been hectic. There'd been a surge of new admissions for some reason, children changing school or moving in to the area, and a number of them had additional funding for special educational needs—so it was my responsibility to check they were settling in okay. One little girl, Dolly, who had a heart condition and could only attend for half days around her treatment, was having real problems settling. She cried for her mum for the first half an hour she was in school each day. Juggling working with Dolly, as well as the other children I'd been assigned to, and the commitment to my own class, had meant it was an incredibly busy time. I don't know how I'd have coped without my teaching assistant, Helen. She was at least as capable as some of the most experienced teachers in the school and would often take over my class whilst I carried out assessments with those children needing extra support.

Will had been accepted on to a fast-track training programme for head teachers, which had two downsides. One being that we were both so busy we hardly had a chance to catch up, and the other that it meant the likelihood of him moving elsewhere to get a headship was an increasing possibility. I'd never been interested in that sort of promotion myself; I loved the special needs aspect of the work and I didn't want to give all that up to become a glorified manager, even if it did mean double the salary.

By the time the night of the spiritualist medium evening came round, I was more than ready for a night out with Will and the others.

'What have you got there?' He gestured towards the bulging brown envelope under my arm as we headed out of school. 'Present from an admirer?' It was Valentine's Day, after all.

'Kind of.' I grinned at the look that crossed his face. 'It's alright, I'm not keeping any secrets from you; as if Sara would give me half the chance. I swear that woman can smell gossip at twenty paces.'

'So, what is it then?'

'Helen was leading the class today and we had little Dolly in with us, so I could carry out a review on her progress at the same time.' I couldn't stop smiling as I spoke. 'The children asked Helen if they could make some Valentine's cards and Dolly wanted to join in. She made me this.' I pulled the card out of the envelope. Dolly had stuck so much stuff on to the front of the card it would never be able to defy gravity and stand up by itself. There was a wooden peg with a face drawn on it, taped to the centre, and strands of hair glued into the middle of a small lake of white adhesive around its head. The peg had been given a felt dress, also secured by copious amounts of glue, and there was enough glitter to keep a ballroom dancer happy for months. Across the top, in wobbly handwriting, were the words *Bestest Teacher*. I wanted to cry every time I looked at it.

'Is that you?' Will grinned. 'I have to say she's got the hair spot on.'

'Git.' I took a pretend swipe at him and then linked my arm through his. 'What about you? Were you late to work this morning opening all your post from hopeless admirers?'

'Nope, just the one card and that was probably from my mum, or worse still, Imogen.' He shuddered. Our colleague was still making her feelings for him obvious, despite the protocol for no romance in the workplace. Perhaps, like me, she'd realised he would be moving on before too long and so was setting the groundwork before he did. She was barking up the wrong tree, though; that much was obvious from his expression.

'Well, let's hope Miss Bone comes through with a message for us tonight, then.' It was daft and far-fetched, but it had been comforting in the six weeks since her death to think we might get the chance to speak to her again, even if it was through a spiritualist medium called Psychic Cyril.

'I've got to stop off here and get a few bits.' Will pulled his arm away from mine as we reached the metro supermarket just down the road from the school. 'But I'll pick you up about seven, if you want to go down to the hall together?'

'That would be great.' I lowered my eyes. 'I know it sounds crazy, but there's something a bit spooky about an evening of trying to contact the dead and I'm not sure I'm up for wandering down there in the dark on my own.'

'No worries, Sara and Meg said they'd meet us down there anyway. So I'll see you later and I can hum *Blackbird* all the way, if it helps? After all, if that doesn't make muggers and dark forces from the underworld give us a wide berth, nothing can!' Will leant forward and kissed me on the cheek. 'And by the way, Kate, you've worked miracles with Dolly. I know I probably don't say it often enough, in a professional capacity that is, but you're one in a million.'

The lobby of the village hall where the spiritualist group held their meetings was buzzing—Psychic Cyril clearly had a big pull. Meg's grandmother was with a group of older people, who she said were regulars at the meetings when she'd come over to say hello. But there was a real span of ages amongst those queuing for coffee and cakes as they waited for the meeting to start.

'Do you want something to eat or a cup of tea?' Will looked towards the line of people waiting to be served and then back to me.

'No, I'm fine.' My stomach was suddenly doing somersaults anyway. The chances of Miss Bone, of all people, coming through and speaking to me from among everyone in the crowd, even if Psychic Cyril wasn't a big, fat fake, were remote at best. But what if she did, and what if she told me I wasn't cut out to be a mother?

'Any sign of the others?' Will's gaze darted around the room. It would have been hard to spot Meg and Sara in the throng, and we'd almost certainly hear Sara before we saw her.

'No, but Sara texted to say she's running late.' I checked my phone again. Nothing from Meg. I felt sure she'd be here first, organising us all and making sure the evening she'd persuaded us to attend ran like clockwork.

'There's Meg!' Will gestured towards another door at the side of the big double doors which led into the main area of the hall. Meg was blotchy and looked hot, despite the cold weather. Maybe she'd been running late, too, and had come in another way to avoid fighting her way through the crowds.

'Do you want me to get you a coffee? You look a bit stressed.' Will said as Meg greeted us both with a kiss.

'I could do with a gin and tonic, actually!' Her hands were shaking. It was freezing outside, but her face felt hot against mine.

'Are you okay?' Her eyebrows did their familiar knitting together thing as I spoke, but she nodded her head quickly.

'I just had a bit of a run in with a supplier, that's all. Had to use all my charm and then stand my ground quite firmly to persuade him to deliver my order.' Meg grimaced. 'He said it was an item he didn't stock, but I knew he did, and it all got a bit heated.'

'Get you, a hard-headed business woman!' I glanced over to the double doors again, where a second queue was starting to form. 'Maybe we'd better leave the gin and tonic until afterwards. It looks like they're about to call us in.'

'Jesus Christ, I thought I wasn't going to make it!' Sara's voice cut across the room and, as predicted, we heard her before we saw her. 'Things are supposed to get easier when your kids grow out of nappies and start being independent, but mine are harder work than they've ever been.' Her breath was coming in short bursts by the time she got over to us and the double doors had been pulled open, so people had begun filing into the hall.

'You can fill us in later.' Meg grabbed hold of mine and Sara's wrists and propelled us into the hall, with Will trailing in our wake. 'I want to get up somewhere near the front.'

She wasn't giving us any choice but to follow her and, in the end, after nearly causing a domino-effect to the pensioners filing slowly into the hall in front of us, we ended up in the third row. The spiritualist group were pretty well organised and, within moments, everyone was seated and the lights were being lowered.

Psychic Cyril strode determinedly on to the stage, which was lit by a single spotlight. He wore a smart suit, but had wispy blond hair that gave him the appearance of a dandelion clock, as though one puff of wind would have sent it billowing up into the rafters. Other than that, he looked fairly normal, rather than paranormal, but since I'd never met a psychic medium before I didn't really know what to expect.

The first twenty minutes passed much as I'd suspected they would, with Cyril making vague guesses along the lines of, "Is there anyone in the audience who knows someone called John?" Of course, almost all of us knew someone called John, so he narrowed it down gradually by adding other factors, like his hair colour and his relationship to audience members, until he had a terrified-looking woman, three rows behind us, convinced her dead brother, John, was sending her a message that it would be a mistake to move to Rhyl to be nearer her grandchildren. I hoped to goodness she ignored him; she looked like she could do with a few cuddles. The thought that she might not get to spend more time with her grandchildren, because some wispy-haired charlatan had told her not to, was horrifying. At least that's what I thought for the next two minutes. Having advised Betty—I think that was her name—to stay put, Cyril wandered up and down the stage telling the audience that the next spirit was trying to get through. He began swaying in an over-exaggerated way, his arms flailing up and down as he moaned.

'Sounds like the spirits know how to show someone a good time.' Sara giggled and earned one of Meg's killer looks. *She* was the natural school teacher among us and I wondered briefly how many times a day she shot filthy looks at the children picking up toys in her shop. She could be good fun, though, and she was the perfect balance to Sara; it was just that she always wanted things to be perfect. She'd suggested the psychic night, after all, and she'd hate it if we all thought it a waste of time. I'd had a good laugh already, though, and in my opinion that could never be considered a waste.

'I've got a message for you!' Suddenly Cyril jabbed a plump finger towards the row where we were sitting, but I couldn't be sure which one of us he was actually pointing to. 'It's from a mother-figure, someone you've turned to for advice over the years.'

'That's about a quarter of the population covered then. Anyone older than us and female,' Sara grumbled under her breath, so as not to earn another dirty look from Meg.

'She's saying something about the colour yellow and telling you to follow the bones to find your way.' Cyril's eyes widened, as if the words he'd said surprised him as much as they had the audience, who were gasping at the mention of bones. 'Does that mean anything to anyone?'

'It means something to us.' Meg stuck her hand up enthusiastically, taking me back almost twenty years. She'd always been the first to volunteer an answer, even back then.

'No, not you!' Cyril shook his head violently. 'Wait your turn, young missy, I'll tell you if there's time.' At the mention of the phrase "young missy", a cold sensation curled around my spine. Miss Bone had always called us that, if we pushed our luck, asked her questions she didn't want to answer, or tried to push for a reading before she was ready. No-one else had ever called me that and I was sure Meg and Sara could say the same. Whichever one of us she wanted to speak to, she was here in the form of Psychic Cyril, I was suddenly sure of it. I would have bet my car on him being a phoney but, to my utter shock, I really believed he was giving us a message from Joan.

'Katherine, it's you I want to talk to.' Cyril was definitely staring at me. Only my mother and Miss Bone had ever called me Katherine since I'd left school, and my scalp prickled in response to the name.

'What does Miss Bone have to tell her?' Sara leapt in with the question, I was so shocked I couldn't find the words. Will, who was next to me on the other side, put his hand over mine. He must have been able to feel me shaking. I'd wanted Miss Bone's advice, but I didn't like this one bit. We were messing with stuff we shouldn't.

'The decision you're thinking of making isn't the right one. I can see you as a mother, but not like that.

It's the wrong path for you, missy.' Cyril was still swaying, his hair billowing like candyfloss in a wind tunnel.

'What's the right one then?' I found my voice at last and managed to squeeze it past the lump in my throat. I had to know what she thought I should do.

'You'll find the answer in red and white.' Cyril was staring straight at me again, but as though he wasn't really seeing me at all; he might have been looking through me and right out the other side.

'What do you mean?' I needed more than that. It was too ambiguous to pin all my hopes on some vague prediction about a combination of colours that made no sense to me at all. Maybe I'd meet the father of my children at an Arsenal match, but then again I didn't like Arsenal, or football come to that.

'She's gone.' Cyril half collapsed on to the stage, and one of the organisers from the spiritualist centre joined him and clapped her hands.

'We'll have a short interval, everyone, whilst Cyril recovers from such a close encounter with the spirit world.' She clapped her hands again to emphasis the point. 'There are refreshments in the foyer and we'll reconvene for the second half in twenty minutes.'

'Well, what did you make of that then?' Sara spoke with her mouthful, half a cup cake wedged into her right cheek, like a hamster about to go into hibernation. 'I thought it was bull at first, but when he started saying missy and calling you Katherine, I actually got goose-bumps.'

'Are you sure someone hasn't been speaking to him, giving him inside information?' Will looked at us questioningly. It was the same look I'd seen him use with kids at the school when someone had knocked the harvest festival display over and no-one had come forward to own up. It was the opposite of *I'm Spartacus*, with all of Year 3 blaming each other.

'Who could give him that information? The only three people who know the details are standing next to me.' The prickling sensation crept across my scalp again. Although I'd agreed to come along, getting advice from Miss Bone was the last thing I'd really expected.

'So what are you going to do now?' Meg's face blanched, all the colour she'd had earlier long since drained away. I knew she'd hadn't wanted me to rush into any decisions, but she didn't seem to be celebrating the visit from Miss Bone any more than the rest of us.

'No idea.' I shrugged. 'See if I can work out what on earth the red and white reference might mean, I suppose. But one thing I do know is that I'm not going back in there for the second half.'

Chapter Six

It was a week before we could all meet again and, sitting in the bar of Belle's, I could tell that Sara and Meg were having to sit on their hands, they were so eager to show me the results of their "red and white" research, as we were now calling it. Only Will was holding back. He thought it was all madness. He'd told me at school, the week after the *contact* with Miss Bone from beyond the grave, that I ought to go for it, take the practical route, seize the moment before it was lost. I was worried about him. He'd been so melancholy of late, so full of advice about not letting that "one moment" pass. I was sure it was all tied up with Louisa, somehow or another, but, if I was honest, I'd had so much on my mind that I hadn't had time to really talk to him about what was bothering him. I'd get onto that, I would, as soon as I'd sorted out what the hell this red and white prophecy was supposed to mean.

'Come on then, spill the beans, I know you're dying to!' I turned to Sara, who'd been ignoring the large glass of white wine in front of her. That in itself was nothing short of a miracle.

'Well, I was thinking about the red and white thing.' She grinned and tucked her blonde hair behind her ears, leaning forward conspiratorially. 'I've been thinking of little else, to be honest, lying awake at night wondering what it might mean, and then it hit me.'

'So are you going to tell us about this revelation, or do we have to guess?' Will, who was already on his second pint, gave her an impatient look.

'St Nicholas Bay High, of course! Our uniform back then was red jumpers with white shirts, remember?' Sara rummaged in her bag and pulled out an envelope. 'Then I found this in an old album at Mum and Dad's: our fifth form photo.' She pulled a picture out of the envelope and passed it across the table. There we all were, the fifty or so of us who'd made up the two fifth form classes back in the late 1990s. I spotted Will immediately in the back row: he'd been one of the tallest in the year, all floppy fringe and futile attempts at a goatee. I scanned the photo looking for the three of us girls and there we were: all together, as we always were, with our Rachel-from-*Friends* haircuts and pouts perfected from hours spent in front of the mirror just practising.

'Oh my God, I'd forgotten half these people!' It was hard to believe the photograph had been taken almost eighteen years before.

'Yeah, but I bet you hadn't forgotten him!' Sara pointed to a boy in the back row, about three across from Will and the object of all my teenage affection—Simon Miller. I was going to marry that boy. He hadn't known it, of course, but Meg and Sara had; we'd wiled away many a happy hour planning my wedding dress and their bridesmaids' outfits. We'd eventually had one slow dance at the end-of-term disco and a quick fumble when he offered to walk me home afterwards. There'd been a bit of hand-in-the-bra action and some fairly frantic kissing and I'd thought it was going to be the start of our great romance at last. Then, that very weekend, I'd caught chicken pox from my cousin, at the grand old age of sixteen and, by the time I returned to school two weeks later, he was going out with Sadie Hardcastle.

'Simon and Sadie have probably got five kids by now.' I smiled at the memory; all that teenage angst had seemed genuinely heart-breaking back then.

'They haven't and he's single, actually.' Sara was looking extremely smug.

'And how do you know all this?' The irritation in Meg's voice was obvious. Whatever "red and white" revelation she had up her sleeve, Sara was delaying it and she clearly wasn't amused.

'It's what Facebook is for, you wally.' Sara winked. 'I'd be extremely good at stalking, should the need ever arise. I've researched all the boys, well, those we aren't already in contact with, of course, and I can tell you exactly who's married, who's divorced and living back at home with their mummy, and even who's doing three years for fraud at Her Majesty's pleasure.'

'Really! Not Simon?' For the first time Will looked animated, but she shook her head.

'No, he's free in both senses of the word.' Sara smirked. 'So what do you reckon, now your pox has cleared up and everything? Could he be the red and white answer to all your prayers?'

'What am I supposed to do, just message him on Facebook and ask if he's looking for love and, oh, by the way, would he be up for getting me pregnant at some time in the next year?'

'I thought we could invite him to one of our Old St Nickers get-togethers?' Sara raised an eyebrow, as if daring anyone to object. No prizes for guessing who did.

'The small get-togethers are just for the committee.' Meg's irritation wasn't dissipating. 'The next get-together for ex-pupils isn't until the annual Halloween party. You know that as well as I do.'

'Well, that's perfect then, because he's working in the States at the moment anyway.' Sara folded her arms, a fait accompli as far as she was concerned.

'How do you know that?' Will, who wasn't a fan of social media, furrowed his brow. 'Is it really that easy to get this kind of information about *anyone*?'

'It was pretty easy for me, I just sent him a message!' Sara gave him a pitying look. 'So what do you think?'

'I think she could almost *make* a baby in the eight months you're asking her to wait!' Meg took the photograph from in front of me and turned it over. End of story, it seemed. 'I've found something else in red and white that's a lot more focused, and you're guaranteed that anyone involved is on the look-out for a relationship.' Meg reached into her bag and passed me a business card with a logo, a white cherub inside a red heart; *Cupid Dating: over-thirties looking for love*.

'Online dating?' My heart sank. I wasn't sure I had the energy or the inclination to try that hard.

'Why not?' Meg drummed her fingers on the table.

'Actually, it's got to be a better idea than waiting to hook up with Simon at the Halloween party. He could be paunchy with half his teeth missing by now.' Will looked decidedly cheered by the thought. 'That's if he even turns up. In fact, if you want some company trying the online stuff out, I might sign up myself.'

I was about to respond, say something to Will about it being a bad idea for him to start up anything new when he was still so hung up on Louisa. But then again, what did I know? It had been three years after all. As it turned out, Meg didn't give me the opportunity.

'Fabulous! Well, I'll set a profile up for you too then, Will, I've already done one for Kate. But we won't mention your terrible singing, or that sticking your tongue out thing you do.' Meg was in her element, which was a pretty scary place to be.

'You've done what?' I wasn't sure whether to laugh or tell her in no uncertain terms that she'd overstepped the mark.

'Well, as everyone keeps saying, the clock is ticking, so I didn't want you procrastinating.'

'What did you put on *my* profile then?' Panic suddenly gripped my insides. Meg had known me since I was four; there were a million embarrassing things she could have included. Although, judging by what she'd said to Will, she was pretty good at filtering the facts. At least it wasn't Sara in charge of my profile; that *would* have been a recipe for disaster.

'Only good stuff.' Meg tapped the side of her nose. 'This has got to be what Miss Bone meant. I knew it as soon as I saw the logo for that website.'

'Well, I for one am insisting on regular meet-ups with you both for updates.' Sara finally took a huge slug of her wine. 'Now, who wants another drink, while we decide exactly what Will should put on his dating profile?'

Chapter Seven

As it turned out, I only had the chance to go on one date, before my life changed for ever and the real red and white revelation presented itself. Will, it seemed, was having far more success.

'Are you off out again tonight?' I cradled my mobile phone between my ear and my shoulder, scooping up my handbag and locking the car door, without having to pause the conversation. It gave a whole new meaning to the expression "hands-free".

'Yes, just trying to decide now if jeans are too casual or whether I can get away with it if we're only going for a drink.' As Will spoke, I suppressed the urge to laugh. I'd never known him to be as indecisive as this over such small things, but then I guess it was a long time since he'd last dated. He'd met Louisa in the first year of uni and that was almost fifteen years ago now—it was a long time to be out of the dating game.

'So is this a second date with Tania?' I slung my bag over one shoulder and took hold of the phone in my other hand, as I crossed the car park. It was a relief for my neck not to be wedged on one side anymore. I wanted to talk to Will, but I couldn't be late for my appointment, so multi-tasking was my only option.

'No, that's tomorrow night. This is a first date with Seraphina, in case tomorrow night doesn't work out.'

'Oh, my God, Will, you're a player! See what this online dating lark has turned you in to?' I couldn't help smiling. He wasn't the sort to string anyone along or deliberately hurt someone's feelings, but it was as though, now he'd decided to date, he was flinging himself into it headlong.

'It's alright, they've both got other *first dates* lined up too. It saves wasting time by having a few options, or so I'm told. I know your date with Gavin didn't go brilliantly, but maybe you ought to try it this way. After all, time definitely isn't on your side.' Will sounded like he was in danger of adding another target to my staff review.

'Well, thanks for that, but I don't think the scattergun approach is going to work for me. Gavin was okay, boring but okay. What I realised was that I didn't want to rush into a relationship just to find an *okay* father for my child, because I was up against a deadline and would have to settle for what I could get it. It made me realise that I didn't want to collar some random stranger to father my child. I want to have a baby with you.'

'With *me*?' Will's voice shot up by at least an octave.

'Well, with all of you, I mean. You, Sara and Meg. Between you, you'll make the perfect second parent. The baby will have a fantastic male role model in you, Sara can bring the fun and the chaos and Meg will bring the stability. I don't want to settle for some bloke who I'm forever tied to, just because my clock's ticking. I've known and loved you lot forever and I'm already tied to you for life. So Gavin just helped me realise that my Plan A was the right plan all along, that's all.'

'So you're going through with the sperm donor thing, despite Miss Bone's advice?' It was much harder to tell what he was thinking when I couldn't see his face.

'I thought you said Psychic Cyril was a fake?' He didn't answer and I didn't have time to wonder what had changed his mind. Until we'd started the online dating thing, he'd been the one pushing me to seize the day. 'Anyway, maybe it was still Miss Bone's influence. I met Gavin through Cupid Dating, with their red and white logo, and it *was* the date that helped me realise what I really wanted. No-one said the sign was going to be blatant, after all.'

'As long as you're sure. There's no going back from this, you know?'

'I know. Give me a call later and let me know how it goes with Seraphina, okay?' I ended the call and, with Will's words ringing in my ears, walked through the automatic doors into the doctor's surgery.

Why is that you'll happily read magazines in a doctor or dentist's surgery that you wouldn't in a million years pick off the shelves of your local newsagent? There I was, waiting for the general health check I'd booked as a precursor to my first appointment at the fertility clinic, thumbing through a dog-eared copy of *Gardener's Monthly*. There was an article on how the garden of a stately home had been returned to its former glory after being all but destroyed in a flash flood. None of the ideas would be workable in the postage stamp-sized garden that came with my ground floor flat. A window box and two planters were all that were needed out there. I put the magazine back on the pile and its shiny cover made for a landslide with the rest of the stack. As I straightened them up, the edge of a printed newsletter caught my eye and I pulled it out from the bottom of the pile. It was from the County Council and I couldn't help but register their red and white logo emblazoned across the top of the first page. Maybe that was why I picked it up. It certainly wasn't the headline about a clash between local councillors and residents over a change to bin day collections. It wasn't even up-to-date, it was from November, and yet I kept turning the pages and there, in the centre of this newsletter I might so easily have missed, was what I'd unknowingly been searching for all along.

The top of page four bore the headline *November: National Adoption Month*. There was a short article about the number of children in the county looking for adoptive homes and some pictures of the sort of children who were waiting to be placed. They were all wonderful, of course, but my eyes were drawn to one little boy—who couldn't have been more than a year old—with a shock of black hair that made him look like he'd been plugged into the electric, distinctive almond-shaped eyes and, of all things, a red and white striped jumper. And, in that moment I knew, whatever forces had brought Miss Bone's message to me, she was right, the answer was in front of me—in red and white.

Chapter Eight

'Do you want us to hang around?' Sara squeezed my arm. 'Let the social worker know exactly what level of support you've got on offer, so they understand you're not trying to do all of this on your own?'

'Thanks, but I think I need to handle this by myself. Plus, you lot are brilliant at tidying up and helping me pick out the right outfit to impress a social worker, but you make the flat look crowded!' It was true: having four adults and a child wedged into the small kitchen at my flat was what you might call intimate. Sara, Meg and Will had all offered to come round when I'd panicked about what the social worker might be looking for during the initial visit to my flat. Now that we'd finished it was cleaner than it had ever been and we'd risk-assessed every possible hazard, from the loose runner in the hallway, which Will had fixed with anti-slip tape, to locking away anything that might be perceived as dangerous, including my collection of cheap white wine. They'd more or less dressed me, to make sure I looked the right balance of sensible and fun. I hoped they'd pulled it off, because inside I was feeling anything but calm and collected. Meg had brought her little boy, Riley, and I kept staring at him, wondering if I was really up to the job of being responsible twenty-four-seven for another person, all by myself.

'If you're sure. I'll shoot off then, but text me as soon as it's over!' Sara kissed me on both cheeks and then turned to the others. 'Are you guys heading off too?'

'I better had, I'm meeting Tania for lunch.' I could have sworn Will was blushing. Things had moved on apace with Tania over the last couple of weeks. We'd just broken up for the Easter holidays and he seemed to be spending every spare minute with her. I was happy for him, of course, but there was just a little niggle there. Probably because I hadn't met her yet. I just hoped to God she wasn't another Louisa. I wanted him to find someone who'd appreciate him, that was all.

'I just want to hang on and have a quick word with Kate about something.' Meg gave Sara a beseeching look, as if silently begging her not to ask any questions and, to my surprise, she seemed in the mood to comply.

'See you later, then. Good luck!' With that, Sara and Will were gone.

'What's up?' I turned to Meg. 'I hate it when you give me that look.' I didn't think I could bear it if she tried to warn me off. I was shaking as it was; any doubts she shared about my ability to cope might just have finished me off.

'Before I say anything, I want you to know that I only did what I thought was best at the time.' She picked Riley up and put him on her hip, as though using him as some sort of shield.

'Whatever it is, please can you just tell me, because I'm about as terrified as I've ever been right now and this isn't exactly helping.' As I spoke, Meg sighed and looked at me for what felt like forever.

'Do you remember at the spiritualist meeting, when I arrived late, I was shaking and said I'd had a row with someone, just before I saw you and Will?' Meg frowned and I nodded, letting her carry on. 'I went to see Cyril and told him I knew he was a fake. I Googled psychics when Nan first told me about him coming to the meeting, to see what we were getting ourselves into, and I saw a picture, the spitting image of him from the flyer Nan had given me, of another medium called Mystic Malcolm and some write-up about how he'd been exposed as a fake at a spiritualist church up in Yorkshire. We had a bit of a row when I went to confront him, but I had an agenda all along. Part of me knew it was wrong, even back then, but I was so desperate for you not to rush into things and make a mistake, that I did it anyway.' There were tears in Meg's eyes, and I clutched the side of the kitchen work surface, my legs losing some of their ability to hold me up.

'Go on.'

'I told him I wouldn't expose him if he promised to say something to you, pretend some message had come through from Miss Bone, to put you off the whole sperm donation thing. I know it was stupid and wrong of me and that you'll probably hate me for it, but I couldn't let you go through with the adoption and everything thinking the red and white stuff was a sign. I told him to make something, anything up, and that must have been what he came up with. The red and white wasn't my idea, but, afterwards, I saw the logo for the dating agency and I seized the chance. I thought Cupid Dating was your best chance of meeting someone, falling in love. You know, doing things the old-fashioned way.'

'It doesn't matter.' Relief flooded my body; it really didn't. Whatever it was that had brought me to this point, chance, luck, fake psychics, a message from beyond the grave, it didn't matter. This *was* the way I was supposed to become a mother, I had no doubt now. 'I know you only ever do the crazy things you do because you want to make things right for us. You're our mother hen, Meg, trying to make everyone's life perfect. I know you're worried, but this *is* perfect for me. When I saw the picture in the newsletter, it was as if I'd found what I hadn't even known I was looking for. Funnily enough I wasn't planning to tell the social worker that my decision to adopt had been influenced by a message from a dead school teacher, so in a weird sort of way this actually makes things a hundred times better.'

'Oh, thank God.' Meg put an arm around me, squashing Riley between us in the embrace. 'And I thought the same, you know. This feels so much more right for you than that donation stuff ever did. Maybe it's because I never knew my dad. But I couldn't let you go through with it without telling you the truth. You're going to be a brilliant mum.'

'Thank you.' My words were muffled by the force of the hug she gave me. I only hoped the social worker, about to decide if I could apply to adopt or not, thought so too.

Mike Turner didn't look like a stereotypical social worker. He was wearing a beaten-up aviator jacket, cowboy boots and enough aftershave to mask the smell of the entire can of *Mr Sheen* that Meg had coated every wooden surface of the flat in.

'So I understand you decided to adopt after seeing an article during National Adoption Month?' Mike gave me a look that suggested he heard this sort of thing all the time from people who had no idea what was really involved. He broke another biscuit in half from the plate in front of him, sending a shower of crumbs all over the coffee table. Meg wouldn't have been impressed.

'I saw an article *from* National Adoption Month, that's right, but it was only a couple of weeks ago, not back in November.' I was stumbling over my words, desperate not to make him think I'd been idly toying with the idea for four months. Now definitely wasn't the time to mention signs or messages from beyond the grave—real or invented.

'So have you had enough time to think it through?' Mike looked at me, waiting for a satisfactory answer, whilst dunking the other half of his biscuit into the mug of tea I'd made him. Who said men couldn't multi-task? It looked like my desire to show him how decisive I felt about adoption might be about to backfire.

'I've been thinking about it for a long time. It was just that the article helped me decide for sure.' It wasn't a lie. I'd been thinking about becoming a mum for a very long time.

'Why not just have a baby yourself? Have there been fertility issues?' Mike scanned the paperwork on his clipboard.

'Not that I know of, but I'm single and whilst I considered some other routes to motherhood,' I cringed, not particularly wanting to share the details with Mike, who was now on his third biscuit, 'I realised that I'm meant to adopt. I saw the article and it was as though my whole reason for being was about doing that.' If it sounded cheesy, I couldn't help it. I wasn't religious at all, but that moment in the doctor's surgery had been the closest thing to a revelation I'd ever felt.

'Yes, I read in your file about you considering the use of a sperm donor.' He smiled and for the first time, I relaxed a tiny bit. There was no judgement there. A man in his job had seen and heard it all before, I'm sure. The girl on the phone, when I'd first rung the number from the newsletter, had been so nice, so kind, that I'd blurted just about everything out to her. Not the red and white stuff, thank God, but my decision to be a mum, seeing Charlie's photo—the little boy in the newsletter—and everything falling into place, making me realise that I didn't want fertility treatment with a donor, I wanted to adopt. 'Can I ask, why now?'

'When I was thinking of trying to get pregnant myself, it was all about the biological clock, getting things in place before I hit the slump that comes with turning thirty-five.' He was nodding as I spoke, as if he could sympathise with my dilemma. 'Now there's not that rush, but I want to be a mum so badly my arms ache and, of course, children like Charlie need a combination of energy and patience. It comes to us all at different ages, I suppose, but for me this feels the perfect age to have the combination of those two things.' I looked down, wondering if I was being too honest.

'That all makes sense.' Mike was definitely thawing, realising I wasn't doing this on a whim. 'You do know the likelihood of you being matched with Charlie himself is very slim?'

'Of course. Even in the best case scenario, by the time I'm approved, it will have been at least a year since that photo of Charlie was taken.' I swallowed, getting ahead of myself. Making an assumption that I'd get as far as being approved. 'If I am lucky enough to get through the panel, I hope Charlie will be really settled in another family by then. In fact he could be now, for all I know. It's just I saw him and knew I wanted to provide a family for someone *like* him.'

'A child specifically with Down's Syndrome?' Mike's eyebrows were uncannily good at asking questions all of their own.

'I think so, or another condition I have some experience in working with.' I twiddled with the ring on my right hand. 'I gave your colleague on the phone a bit of a potted history of my life story, so I expect you know I've been working with children with special needs for a number of years and I really think a child *like* Charlie,' I emphasised the word again, 'could be a good match with me.'

'Excellent. Well, we can focus on those skills when we begin the assessment process.' Mike was back to smiling and I almost hugged him. For the first time he'd said the word "when" and not "if". 'I wanted to ask you about relationships. You've said you're single, but do you think the prospect of beginning a new relationship is a possibility?'

'No. I've got a great support network, but I want to concentrate on being a mum, so I really can't see anyone coming along to change that.' It was weird having this sort of conversation with a total stranger, but I knew it was a necessity. I was going to have to tell this man *everything*—I was also going to have to keep the biscuit tin well stocked.

'That's good to know because, if you were to begin another relationship, we'd have to halt the assessment process. We'd need to assess you as a couple, but then only after you'd been together long enough for us to consider your relationship stable which can, in some cases, mean years.'

'It's not an issue.' Finally I took a biscuit, glad we'd moved on to a subject I was certain of. I was going to be a mum and I wouldn't let anything or *anyone* stand in my way.

Chapter Nine

As I'd expected, the assessment process was draining, intrusive and had brought up issues I'd long since buried. But now it was happening, I could think about almost nothing else. I suppose it was like Meg told me: when she was pregnant, she'd suddenly noticed how many other people were pregnant and all she could think about, or wanted to talk about, was the baby. I tried not to bore the others to death, but I spent some time in class during the summer term teaching the children about different types of families—there were some children from step-families in the class and one little boy who lived with his grandparents—and, when we spoke about fostering and adoption, I could feel my excitement growing all the time. It was scary to think that my fate lay in the hands of a panel of strangers I'd be facing in October, all being well with the assessment and it hitting the six-month timescale that Mike had outlined. I watched the children in my class, wondering if my child would have any of the traits or mannerisms they had, like Chloe who always did a strange sort of cross-legged dance when she needed to use the toilet, or Billy who used one arm to push the other one upwards, so his would always be the highest when the children's hands shot up to answer a question.

By the time we were ready to break up for the long summer holiday, so much of myself was invested in adopting a child like Charlie that I had no idea how I would cope if the panel turned me down. So I took the only available option and buried my head in the sand about that possibility.

'What are your plans for the summer, then?' I saw Will's face properly for the first time in what seemed like ages, as he poured us both a cup of coffee on the last day of term. It had been a scarily busy time for both of us and I knew I hadn't offered him as much support as I could have done; in fact I'd probably added extra strain. Fiona, the head, had gone off on long-term sick leave at just the point when the school had been due an inspection. Will had carried the burden for the whole management team in her absence and still let me have all the time off I need to attend training sessions and adoption assessments, to give me the best possible chance of getting through the panel. But now that I looked at him, I mean *really* looked, he was exhausted. 'I hope you've got something relaxing planned, because you look like you need it.'

'Thanks!' Will smiled as he handed me the cup. 'I'm going to Wales, actually, at least for part of the holiday. There are some old friends of ours getting married.' There was an involuntary twist in my gut at the use of the word "ours" in relation to him and Louisa. 'And there are a few other things I need to finalise while I'm down there.'

'The divorce?' It was none of my business, but I couldn't pretend I wasn't glad Louisa was out of Will's life and, as a consequence, out of mine. 'I'm sorry things didn't work out with Tania in the end, either.'

'Umm… I sometimes think only another teacher could put up with dating someone who has to bring as much work home as I do. What about you, what are up to?'

'I'm doing a few more training courses and the summer camp with the children from the visual impairment unit I did my work experience with. You remember, I go every year.'

'Yes, that's right, but what about some relaxation time? This could be your last holiday without someone else to think of.' There was a catch to Will's voice and I couldn't work out why. No-one could have been more supportive, as a boss or a friend.

'Sara said she might be able to get a long weekend off from chauffeuring and chef's duties with the twins, we're thinking of heading to Paris. It's not exactly child friendly, so I thought we'd have one last trip there while we can.' I grinned as the expression on his face changed. We'd been there as a group a couple of times, the first time with the school when we were all sixteen, just before Miss Bone had started imparting her advice and before my stalled romance with Simon Miller. It was the one and only time I thought that Will and I might be something other than friends. Being on top of the Eiffel Tower must have done it—romance in the air and all that. We'd exchanged the briefest of kisses. It was so sweet and half of me hadn't wanted it to end there, but our classmates were only around the other side of the Tower, not to mention the teachers, and so that had been it. Neither of us had ever mentioned it again, but I couldn't hear the word Paris without thinking about it.

'Sounds great. Well, think of me trudging through rainy Welsh valleys whilst you two are sipping champers on the Champs Elysees, won't you?'

'I'll try to recall who you are.' I leant forward to sneak another kiss, but this time only on the cheek. 'Thanks for everything, you've been a star.' Maybe it was just the memory of Paris, but I had a strange feeling of melancholy when I thought of being there without him and realised with a stab that a summer without Will would be a long one. Suddenly a wet, Welsh valley sounded quite tempting.

Chapter Ten

'How was Paris?' Will took the drink I handed him and placed it on the table next to the cardboard box I'd just rescued from the top shelf of my study.

'It was great. Sara emailed some photos over this morning and it got me thinking about the times when we went before. So I thought I'd see if I could dig out the old pictures.' I swept my hand across the dusty lid of the box. 'I've got to put together an album for if I get matched with a child; it helps with the bonding apparently. But I want to make a scrapbook too, so I can talk to them about my life before they came along. I could have done with you turning up ten minutes earlier, actually. It's okay being short, but it's a pain when you've got shelves you can only reach by standing on your desk.'

'Let's have a look then.' Will pulled the box towards him and lifted off the lid. As bad luck would have it, the first photograph was of him and Louisa at their engagement party. He was holding her hand, but she stood away from him—in a sort of dropped-hip model pose—as though she'd always known she might need to crop him out of the photo at a later date.

'God, sorry.' I snatched the photo off the pile. 'I haven't been through these in years, not since I got a digital camera and stopped having to go down to Boots to get them printed out. I don't suppose there's anything less than ten years old in there.'

'Honestly, it doesn't bother me. I saw her a few times when I was in Wales and we were fine.' He gave a rueful shrug. 'In fact, we probably get on better now than we ever did when we were together.'

'Is she seeing someone else?' For some reason I was holding my breath.

'No, well, she wasn't over the summer anyway.' He didn't elaborate. I wanted to ask him if they were involved again, only I didn't want to hear the answer. Louisa had been a mistake and, if I had my way, it wasn't one I wanted him to repeat—but it wasn't my life.

'Look at this! Your hair was something else back then. What was it called again, road kill?' Will held up a photograph of the four of us in Paris, just after Sara had started a part-time hairdressing course which she'd abandoned soon after. For some stupid reason, I'd agreed to let her practice on me, and I'd ended up with thick blonde streaks in the centre of my hair and the sides had been cut so short they almost looked like they'd been shaved. Will was right: looking back, I did look like I was sporting a squashed badger on my head.

We'd been in Paris for his unofficial stag do and we'd gone back to the same hotel where we'd spent our school trip ten years earlier. Sara's mum had stepped in to have the twins for the weekend, so Joe wouldn't be left to cope alone and Sara could come too, and Meg had been the fourth Musketeer. Will had been given a boys' do back in Wales, too, which had ended up with him losing an eyebrow and very nearly his fiancée, only, sadly, it hadn't quite done the trick. But the trip to Paris had meant more to him, he'd told us as much at the time. Will passed me another photo. 'Trust Sara to get up to this sort of thing.'

'I'm surprised we didn't end up getting deported!' The picture was taken on top of the Eiffel Tower and

Sara was wearing a string of plastic onions around her neck. She'd pulled the same trick on the school trip ten years before and ended up getting a week's detention for it when we got back home. I'd been glad of the laughs on both trips though. That first time, when Will and I'd kissed, and then it was like it had never happened. It was easier to pretend it hadn't with Sara larking about and playing the fool, less embarrassing all round than acknowledging it or asking Will how he felt about me. And then, on his stag do, when we were up there again, I'd really wanted to ask him if he was sure about Louisa, tell him it wasn't too late to change his mind. Sara's antics had broken the tension and I'd bottled out, relieved to have an excuse not to.

'Have you got any from when we went there with the school?' Will sifted through a few more photos, and I shook my head.

'I thought I did, but they must be in Mum and Dad's loft. I can see some in there from when we were at school, which she must have given me, but none of that French trip; most of them seem to be from when we were in our twenties. I'll have to have a look next time I'm up at their place.'

We looked through some more pictures. There was our last day at school, when we'd all signed each other's shirts and vowed never to lose touch. I suppose all school leavers feel that way, saying goodbye to the friends they've spent almost every day with for the last seven years and, for those of us who'd been at primary school together, it had been twice as long. Only we really did stay friends, bonded by something stronger than our shared experiences and the close-knit community of the Bay.

There were parties, university graduations—mine and Will's—high days and holidays. There were a couple of photographs, which looked like they'd been in frames at one time and had slightly faded in the sun, of Will and I digging on the beach when we were toddlers, and another one of us pulling a Christmas cracker, clearly quite a competition, aged about eight. There was one right at the bottom of the pile, I think it must have been a birthday party—although I can't remember whose now—in the back garden of my parents' house. Two of the fence panels had been taken down between our house and Will's and you could clearly see the barbecue going in one garden and drinks being poured in the other. We'd had a few of those parties over the years and we'd taken it for granted, at least I had, having some of our best friends living right next door and the rest of them elsewhere in the Bay. It had been idyllic, and I suppose it was the reason the Bay got under your skin in a way you couldn't explain to any outsider. It was what I wanted for my child more than anything. So what Will said next took me by surprise.

'Do you ever think about moving?' He was putting the photos back in the box as he spoke, so I couldn't see the expression on his face.

'From the flat, do you mean, or *really* moving?'

'I guess the flat, but the Bay too, I suppose. Property prices are shooting up and I sometimes wonder if I couldn't buy a heck of a lot more if I moved elsewhere.' Will shrugged, as if it were a casual off-the-cuff remark, but I knew him too well for that.

'I can't think of anywhere else I'd want to live.' I wanted to tell him that if he was thinking of leaving the Bay to please Louisa, that it wouldn't ever be enough—after all, he'd said as much himself—only I didn't. Putting the lid back on the box, I just prayed that Miss Bone had been right, and that Will would realise he couldn't be happy anywhere else but home, in the Bay, with the people who really loved him.

Chapter Eleven

'Are you nervous?' Will turned to face me, as he brought the car to a halt in the car park outside an innocuous looking building, inside of which my fate and my chance at motherhood were about to be decided. My hands were shaking so much, I had to put one on top of the other to hold them steady.

'About as terrified as I've ever been.' I tried to smile, but didn't quite manage it. My stomach was churning and all I wanted was for it to be two hours later, when I knew, either way, the decision would be made and it would all be over.

'I could always sing to you, if you like?' He grinned, but I shook my head.

'Tempting as that offer is, I'd better learn to cope without it. After all, if it all works out, I've got to be the grown-up taking someone to their first day at school one of these days, so I better learn a few soothing songs myself.'

'Do you want me to come in with you, or shall I wait here?' Will had driven me to the adoption panel and I wasn't sure I could have made it without him. It was the end of October and the half-term holiday, but we'd both had to duck out of the preparations for the Old St Nickers biggest event of the year, the annual Halloween party. Thankfully Sara, Meg and the others had stepped in to share the load.

'Whatever works best for you. I've got to meet my social worker inside anyway, so if you need to do something in town, I can text you after?' I was holding on to that. There *would* be an after— whatever happened.

'I do need to check out a couple of estate agents.' Will didn't look at me, and I wasn't ready for a conversation about anything else life-changing at that moment. The adoption panel was in Eascourt, a market town about fifteen miles inland from St Nicholas Bay. It was home to several chains of estate agents that covered sales in the Bay, so it would make sense if Will was really thinking about selling up. He'd seemed unsettled since after the summer holidays. Fiona had returned to work, so he'd been forced to relinquish the temporary headship he'd worn so well in her absence. It wasn't just that, though; he'd been preoccupied, as though he was with us in body but his mind was somewhere else. He hadn't said much more about his trip to Wales, other than what he'd told me when we were sorting through the old photos at my flat, except that it had been nice to catch up with old friends. I'd avoided saying any more about Louisa, she wasn't a comfortable topic of conversation for either of us, but something had to have happened. Will would tell me when he was ready; I'd known him long enough to be certain that pushing him would only delay that moment. Maybe moving house would be what he needed. A new start out of the place he'd shared, albeit very temporarily, with his wife. As long as he stayed in the Bay. Anything else I couldn't contemplate.

'Okay, well, I'll text you then.' I leant against his chest, wishing that I didn't have to leave and face the panel.

'Good luck, Kate, not that you'll need it.' In the end, Will was the one to draw away, and I opened the car door, taking the next very scary step towards my future.

'Are there any further questions from the panel?' The chair of the meeting had honey-blonde hair and a ready smile. She'd made me feel comfortable from the outset and, up until that point, none of the questions from the panel members had thrown me. Why did I want to adopt? Why a child with additional needs? What plans did I have for returning to work? How would I manage to include a suitable male role model in my support network? Will's name came up more than once.

'There's just one other thing I wanted to ask.' A dark-haired man, whose name I had completely forgotten, smiled across the table at me. I think he'd said something about being an adopter himself, or maybe an adoptee. Either way, it looked like he might be about to ask me the final question which stood between me and the panel's decision. 'I wanted to ask you about relationships.'

'You mean with my support network?' I felt my brows knit together, in what must have been a passable impression of Meg. I'd already answered that question once.

'No. I mean the chance of you starting a new relationship.' The dark-haired man smiled. 'You're still young, with a chance for birth children, so I was just wondering if you saw the possibility of a new relationship in your future.'

'Oh, no.' I swallowed hard, as I watched his eyebrows shoot up in surprise. It was the same question Mike had asked me all those months ago and my answer hadn't changed. 'I mean, obviously no-one knows exactly what's around the corner, but it definitely isn't something I'm thinking of or actively looking for. A new relationship really isn't a priority, at least not with anyone but the child who's placed with me, if I'm lucky enough to be approved.'

'Excellent, because any child placed with you will need to go through a bonding process, and the instability that can come with new relationships is unlikely to provide the best environment for that to take place. Certainly, any relationship that started after approval, should that be the case, would almost certainly have an impact on the likelihood of you being matched with a child.'

'I understand and it really isn't a problem.' I smiled. Please let this be it, no more questions.

'Well, I think we've got all the information we need to help us make our recommendation. If you could wait outside briefly, the panel will have a further discussion and then call you in to hear our decision.' That was it; within minutes the panel would decide whether to recommend me to adopt. There was nothing further I could do.

✉ from: Kate
Hi Will. All finished. Where are you? Kate x

✉ from: Will
Already waiting outside? So, COME ON, what's the verdict? X

✉ from: Kate
We can talk about it in the car⋯ x

I'd tried to be coy, but I'd never been big on keeping secrets, and I should have known the result would be written all over my face. By the time I was halfway across the car park, Will had leapt out of his car. My smile, plastered from cheek to cheek, had given the game away. Will swept me into his arms and swung me around.

'I knew it! They'd have been idiots not to approve you!' For a moment, our eyes locked.

'You better put me down, in case they're watching.'

'Why, do you think they might change their minds if they see you irresponsibly swinging around in a car park?'

'Being in your arms is the big risk. They kept reminding me that the panel just makes a recommendation, and that the local authority decision-maker has the final say. They also warned me off starting new relationships again, as it might jeopardise me being matched with a child, once my approval is finalised.' I smiled at the look on his face. 'You might only be one of my best friends, but there's a chance they could look out here and get the wrong end of the stick.'

'*Only* one of your best friends? I thought that was a pretty exclusive club.'

'It is.' I grinned again, nothing was going to keep me down. 'And we'd better go and help the other members of that club carve out some jack-o'lanterns, and give them the news, or our lives won't be worth living!

It always amazed me how the school hall at St Nicholas Bay High could be transformed by the boxes of Halloween decorations that Meg stored in her loft between the celebrations each year, and a few carved pumpkins. The boxes contained an Aladdin's cave of All Hallows' Eve trinkets, from rubber zombie arms to bat-wing bunting and almost everything in between. Sara was the Old St Nickers treasurer and she went on a shopping spree every first of November to see what decorations she could pick up for the following year at a knockdown price. The previous November she'd snapped up a smoke machine and an inflatable ghost. The celebrations themselves had changed over the years too. We'd started out as a group of mainly singletons, with nothing better to do than drink punch out of a giant plastic skull, but now there were children to consider and so most of the alcohol had given way to apple bobbing and pin the tail on the devil, but it was still just as much fun.

As luck would have it, Luke, one of the Old St Nickers from the year below was the caretaker at the school, so we never had to worry about waiting to be let in and rushing to get everything ready. By the time Will and I made it to the High School, after the adoption panel, most of the decorations were up. Meg and Sara were being helped out by Jas and Rosie, who'd been in the year below us, and it seemed they'd already sampled a glass or two of the punch. There was a serious amount of giggling going on, and Sara was chasing an unusually relaxed Meg around with the rubber zombie arm.

'At last!' Sara whipped round and almost took my eye out with the zombie's outstretched fingers.

'We've been dying for news and we had to have a drink to calm our nerves!'

'Not before Meg made sure we'd hung all the decorations straight though.' Rosie laughed in a good natured way. All of the Old St Nickers gang knew about the adoption panel and I'd been getting good luck texts from them all day.

'So, come on then, what's the news?' Meg launched herself at me and the smile, which had been twitching at the corners of my mouth all the way home, gave the game away yet again.

'They said yes?' I nodded as Sara and Meg almost knocked me flying.

'I'm going to be a mum.' My voice was muffled, but hearing the words out loud somehow made them real.

'All the more reason to celebrate.' Jas held up a cup of something red and fizzy that she'd scooped out of the skull. 'Brain juice, anyone?'

I'd been round to my parents and told them about the panel's decision, after we'd got the last of the preparations sorted at the High School, which meant I only had half an hour to get ready for the party. Not that I cared; the day had been amazing, my parents had both cried, and I knew whatever child was eventually placed with me, he or she would be lucky to have them for grandparents. Mum was already fussing about their Christmas cruise, asking if she should cancel it, so that they didn't miss their grandchild's first Christmas with us. There was no way I was letting them do that, though. There was no guarantee I'd even be matched with a child by then, and if I let them cancel their holiday it was bound to tempt fate and I'd end up not getting a placement at all. It was silly and superstitious, but it was the way I felt. Luckily, I persuaded Mum in the end, mostly because Dad had looked like a lost child himself at the thought of missing out on his Christmas cruise with Will's parents. There'd be plenty of family Christmases from here on out, so one last cruise wasn't going to hurt anyone.

I changed quickly into the Bride of Frankenstein outfit that I'd worn the year before. Sara and Meg were both brilliant at coming up with something new each year and, usually, I made the effort too, but this year time seemed to have run away with me. Walking into the school hall, the first person I saw was Will. He was dressed as a werewolf and looked pretty scary, despite which he was surrounded by children and was organising the *piñata*, a giant black papier-mâché spider. Unlike me, Will had always planned to be a teacher; kids gravitated towards him and I knew he missed the teaching now that he was in a managerial role and spent far less time in the classroom.

Will turned and smiled and, as he did so, a figure behind him honed into view. It was Simon Miller and the memory of that one dance with him, in the very same hall, came flooding back. My teenage years had been a series of near-misses, first the kiss with Will in Paris, and then the dance with Simon. Will had been in my life ever since, which he probably wouldn't have been if we'd ever ended up going out, so I couldn't regret that. Simon, however, was one regret I'd never quite shaken and I could still hear Sara offering forth her rationale that our old school uniform might have been the real red and white sign.

Of course, by then I knew Psychic Cyril was really a fake and that something else had led me down the path to motherhood, but that didn't stop Simon being every bit as gorgeous as he'd always been. What's more, his eyes had locked on mine and he'd crossed the room in about six paces.

'Katy-Kat Harris!' Simon used my old nickname and the years peeled away. Kissing me on both cheeks, he stood back and looked me up and down. 'Still the best looking girl at St Nicholas Bay High, with those hazel eyes I could never say no to.'

'Even dressed as the Bride of Frankenstein?'

'Absolutely. Black lips and Mallen streaks have always done it for me.'

'I wish I'd known that back when we were sixteen.'

'There were a lot of things I wish I'd known back then.' Simon took my hand, as if we'd only seen each other the last time a day or so before, instead of almost sixteen years earlier. 'Drink?'

We took our glasses of "brain juice" out of the main hall and into the gym next door. There were a few tables set up in there for anyone wanting to escape from the Haunted House remix, with the *Monster Mash* and *Time Warp* playing on what felt like a non-stop loop.

'You really do look good, you know?' Simon had a way of looking at me that made me feel like the only Bride of Frankenstein in the room, yet something told me it was well practised.

'Hmm. You don't look any different, which is entirely unfair.' It was true, he'd barely aged a day in sixteen years. 'What have you been up to that's kept you looking so young, and what tempted you to finally make it back here to an Old St Nickers' do?'

'I've been in the States, mainly. I worked in London for a bit, in finance, and then got a transfer to New York; it's a great place to live.' Now that he came to mention it, he did have a slight twang and I vaguely recalled Sara having said something about him working in America. 'As for the age defiance, I've got a client who's a plastic surgeon, so we swap expertise—you know, financial advice for a bit of Botox.' I think I must have grimaced, even though I was trying not to judge him when he'd been honest enough to tell me. Call me old school, but there was something a bit off-putting about the kind of guy who had regular Botox when he wasn't even out of his thirties. It was such a contrast to Will, who still seemed exhausted, even after the long summer break. I just hoped he wasn't tired of St Nicholas Bay and all that went with it.

'Sounds like a great deal.' I kept my voice light. 'So don't tell me you've come all the way back here just to attend a Halloween disco in your old school hall.'

'Well, Sara did send me about twenty emails insisting that I had to come; something about fate and fortune telling?' He tried unsuccessfully to raise an eyebrow, but it moved just enough for me to get the point.

'And you hopped on a plane on the basis of that?' My eyebrows had no trouble at all shooting up into my fringe.

'Not exactly. I had some meetings in London this week, but I couldn't miss the opportunity of catching up with everyone, while I was so nearby, just to see what all the fuss was about.' He placed a hand on my arm. 'And now that I've seen you, I'm really glad I did.'

'So, I take it you're still single?' It was more a case of something to say, than being interested. It wasn't just the Botox paralysing his face, it felt like wasted time being with him when I could have been with the Old St Nickers in the next room.

'Yes, still footloose and fancy free, and I gather from Sara that there's no Mr Right waiting at home with two-point-four kids for you, either?'

'No, no Mr Right.' I sighed. Sara had been doing her best to fulfil the red and white prophecy when she'd been emailing Simon, but I suddenly wished I could invent a strapping six-foot husband. Although I had a feeling giving him the news that I was about to become a mother might cause an even stronger reaction. 'I've had some great news today, though. I've been accepted as an adoptive parent.'

'Really?' Simon was so surprised that his eyebrow almost managed an arch. 'Why?'

'Why? Because I spend my days surrounded by great kids, but when I go home there's no-one. I want the chance to be a mum and somehow this just feels like the right way for me to do it.'

'Right. But what if you meet someone later, won't you regret not waiting?' He sounded like he was singing from Meg's old hymn book, but there was far less desire on my part to justify my decisions to him.

'No, not at all. I'm not looking for a relationship and, even if by some fluke it did happen, anyone I met would have to want us both, as part of a package. There are hundreds of children waiting for a family, especially those with disabilities or special needs, so if not now, then when?'

'You're adopting a child with special needs?' He said the words as though they were something dirty, something to be ashamed of. 'Why don't you at least wait for a *normal* child?'

'Look, it's been... interesting catching up with you.' I couldn't bring myself to use the word "good", but it had been another catalyst. I was now a million per cent sure I'd been right not to be persuaded by Meg to wait for Mr Right. If Mr Right was anything like Simon, I'd had a narrow escape and I wasn't going to waste another minute on him. 'But I've got to go.'

'Of course.' He might have looked relieved, but it was difficult to tell. 'Well, good luck with the special kid and all that, although rather you than me.'

'What's up?' Will caught hold of my arm as I moved to dash past him. I needed to get outside but he wasn't letting me go.

'I've had a night of things. First Simon Miller telling me that I should wait to adopt a *normal* child.' I attempted to laugh, but made a strange hollow sound instead. 'And then I had a text from Mike with more news and I can't quite get my head around it. I think I might be in shock.'

'Mike?' Will had removed the werewolf mask and confusion clouded his face; the music blaring all around us wasn't helping either.

'Do you want to come outside with me for a minute, so I can explain? I feel like I need some air.' Will released his grip on my arm as I spoke and placed his hand in the small of my back instead.

'Come on then, I need to get out too. Or I might be tempted to wipe that smug smile off Miller's face.'

'You might need an antidote to Botox first.' We took the side exit out of the hall, onto the netball pitches marked out on the tarmac, illuminated by the security light. The cold hit my throat and seemed to suck some of the air out of my lungs, but it still felt good to be outside, away from Simon and all the noise. I needed a chance to let things sink in.

'I always thought he was a total idiot, even back when we were at school, but for him to make a comment like that. I've never hit someone, but right about now...' There was a muscle pulsing in Will's cheek. 'And who the hell's Mike?'

'Don't let Simon bother you. There are far too many idiots like him about for us to rise to the bait every time one of them says something stupid.' I smiled. 'I love you for caring, though.' Even as I said it, the smile melted from my face. I didn't just love him for caring. I loved Will for everything about him, even his terrible singing. All those photos back at the flat—all my happy memories—had him in them.

Oh my God. I *loved* Will. How had I been so blind for so long? I seemed to lose the power of speech. Not now, please. I shook my head, as though that might change things, as though I could go back to ignorant bliss.

'And Mike?' He turned to me, cupping a hand under my chin so I had to look at him.

'He's my social worker.' It was all I could manage to say. If I'd been in shock after Mike's text, the realisation that my feelings for Will weren't what they should have been had turned my legs to jelly.

'God, yes, sorry. I'd forgotten that was his name. Is everything okay?'

'He texted to say there might be a match for me.' I wanted to lean on Will, but I couldn't. I couldn't risk crossing the line and losing our friendship, it meant far too much to me.

'Already. Wow, no wonder you're in shock. That was much quicker than I thought.'

'Me too, and there's something else. You remember Charlie, the little boy whose photo sparked all this off?' I paused as Will nodded his head. 'Well, apparently he's still waiting to be matched with a family. He's been in foster care all this time, and they think I might be the one with the skills needed to give him a family of his own.'

'But that's brilliant!' Will was beaming and I bit my lip, wishing I could give Charlie a dad like Will. 'Just as well Simon turned out to be a total arse. You wouldn't have wanted a new relationship to put a spanner in the works, not after all the warnings they gave you.'

'You're right, I wouldn't.' I bit my lip again. If I'd been tempted to tell Will how I felt, he'd given me every reason not to. Charlie was my priority right now, assuming the matching panel agreed we'd make a good family. I couldn't risk that for anyone, not even Will. In any case, it was far better to have him in Charlie's life as a father figure, than to scare him off altogether by telling him I loved him, when all he wanted was to be my friend.

'I think it's wonderful, Kate. Like it was meant to be, and Miss Bone really did have something to do with it.' Will grinned and I let myself relax. He was right, it was going to be okay; the important stuff was all falling in to place and the rest would blow over. After all, Miss Bone would have told us way back when if she saw us ending up together and now it was too late to ask—too late in so many ways.

Chapter Twelve

The matching panel was relatively painless, but I still thought I might pass out when the Chair told me they were going to support the recommendation that Charlie should be placed with me. After that, it became a crazy whirlwind of introductions and contact visits, to make sure he'd have the best chance of settling with me. On the last Saturday in November, he spent the night at my flat for the first time. It was the final stage before the placement was formalised and I could begin the process of legally adopting him. By the twenty eighth, Charlie had moved in full time, I'd started nine months of adoption leave and all we had to wait for was the courts to legalise everything.

The flat had been transformed. There were toys everywhere and the spare bedroom—well, Charlie's room, I couldn't call it "spare" any more—had metamorphosed from a storage area to a cosy cream bedroom, with a teddy bear theme throughout and the same beautiful wooden handmade cot that had been mine as a baby.

'Darling, is it okay to come in?' My mother had a key, but she was calling softly through the letter box. My parents had been wonderful about backing off to give me some bonding time with Charlie, even though I knew they were desperate to spend time with him too. Luckily, that bond I'd felt looking at his photograph in the doctor's surgery, almost nine months earlier, was ten times as powerful in real life. Charlie had given me an appraising look at our first meeting and held out one of the plastic shapes he was busy trying to post through the right slots in the toy in front of him, in the middle of the living room floor at his foster carers' house. They'd done a brilliant job with him and he was bright and affectionate and on track developmentally in almost all areas except his speech, despite the Down's Syndrome.

'Of course,' I opened the door and Mum stood there beaming, a bulging bag in each hand, 'is Dad with you?'

'No, I was just in town, getting an early start on some Christmas shopping for Charlie and I went into Tiny Tim's Toys just as Meg was closing up, so we thought we'd pop up on the off-chance.' As Mum spoke, Meg emerged from behind the open door.

'Are you hiding?'

'No, nothing like that. We just didn't want to disturb you, if you were having some quality time with Charlie.' Meg had a large bag emblazoned with the Tiny Tim's logo too. At this rate, Charlie was going to have more toys than Prince George, in a flat that was probably smaller than one of the bathrooms at Buckingham Palace.

'It's fine, he's having a nap actually.' I laughed as Mum's face fell. 'But it would be lovely to have a coffee and catch up with you both.'

Mum and Meg were chatting easily in the lounge when I brought the drinks and a coffee and walnut cake through.

'Did you make that?' The expression on Mum's face made me smile again.

'Yep, I'm turning into quite the domestic goddess of late. It must be motherhood.'

'Well, it suits you.' Meg mirrored my smile. 'Is everything as rosy as it looks?'

'It is.' This smiling thing had been hard to rein in since Charlie had arrived. Life was perfect, well, maybe not quite perfect, but certainly closer to it than anyone had the right to expect. 'I can't believe how much I love it. How's everything with you? Has the Christmas rush started at the shop yet?'

'It has, and your mum has done a pretty good job of getting it going!' Meg took the slice of cake I'd cut for her. 'Riley already has twenty-three things on his Christmas list, so make the most of Charlie not quite knowing what's going on yet. I've brought him one of my wooden advent trees, though; it's got a little toy in each of the boxes that hang from the branches.' She lifted the beautiful handcrafted wooden Christmas tree out of the bag she'd brought in.

'My *son*,' the word still amazed me, 'is going to be the luckiest little boy in St Nicholas Bay with the friends and family we've got.'

'He already is.' Mum and Meg spoke in unison. 'Having you as a mum.'

'Ooh, spooky! Did you practice that on the way over?' I took a forkful of cake. It tasted pretty good, even if I did say so myself.

'No, and it's not the first spooky thing that's happened to me today.' Meg met my gaze and two perfectly round spots suddenly coloured her cheeks. 'Does your mum know about the Psychic Cyril thing?'

'Yes, Kate told me all about it. Hilarious really and pretty cunning of you, but all's well that ends well.' Mum leant towards Meg and spoke in a loud stage whisper. 'In fact, I'm jolly glad, because I wasn't sure about that whole donation thing and we wouldn't have got our gorgeous Charlie otherwise.'

'Well, that's the thing, I'm not sure I had a hand in any of this after all.' Meg set the coffee cup down on the table in front of her. 'Nan came into the shop this morning, to ask me to put a poster in the window for another psychic night for the spiritualist group, and I got a bit cross about them using Psychic Cyril again after last time, what with him being a known phoney and everything.'

'I bet that didn't go down well.' Meg shook her head as I spoke, we were both well aware that her grandmother was passionate about her beliefs.

'Well, that's the thing. She admitted that Cyril *used* to be a fake.'

'Used to be?' Mum's fork hovered in the air as she spoke and she'd taken the words right out of my mouth.

'He confessed that until the meeting in February, it was all just guess work. But then, that night we all went along, he said he genuinely heard a voice telling him what to say for the first time ever.' Meg's eyebrows had gone to their default setting of knitting together. 'Nan and her friends grilled him pretty hard before agreeing to book him again, but he insisted that a voice calling herself Joan had told him to say those things and it scared him half to death, by all accounts. For a long time he thought about giving up all together, but ever since then he's been getting no end of messages from the other side and now he's got no choice.'

'And what's to say he's not lying now?' It didn't matter to me and, even if Cyril had made the whole thing up, I was glad he had. Subconsciously, I think it *was* the red and white connection that had made me pick up the newsletter, and now I had my Charlie because of it.

'Nothing, I suppose, but Nan seemed convinced. Said he knew things he couldn't have known otherwise. They asked him questions that only people no longer with us would know the answers to.' Meg shrugged. 'I just wanted you to know.'

'Maybe we should book Will into the next session. He doesn't seem himself lately and Janice is really worried about him.' Mum sighed. She'd been best friends with Will's mum since before either of us were born, and I knew they discussed us both far more than I felt comfortable with.

'He'll be okay when he gets all this divorce stuff finalised.' I metaphorically crossed my fingers that it *would* be as simple as that, and for a moment my happiness was tinged with something else. I missed seeing Will every day, and it was good for us to have some distance –good for me at any rate—but I hated the idea of not being there for him if he needed me. The sound of Charlie stirring on the baby monitor set the lights flashing and Mum's face lit up too, everything else temporarily forgotten.

Chapter Thirteen

Preparing for Christmas with a child in the house was everything I'd dreamed it would be. So there were no cocktails with Meg and Sara and no Christmas do with my colleagues from school, and Will of course. But being up to my knees in wrapping paper, and having a table that was suddenly more craft glue than wood, more than compensated. Charlie and I made Christmas cards for everyone I knew. He was from the Jackson Pollock school of painting and admittedly more paint ended up on him than on the cards but, given that he was still three months off his second birthday and I was completely biased, I think he showed considerable talent.

The look on his face when I plugged in the fairy lights on the tree made the fact I could only hang baubles from the middle up all part of the charm. He still grabbed at the lower branches once or twice, but without the sparkly baubles as temptation, and with only a handful of scratchy pine needles as a reward, he soon went off the idea.

Charlie loved being pushed around St Nicholas Bay in his buggy. No one could resist his big brown eyes and toothy grin and it took twice as long to get anywhere because people would stop and chat to us. He didn't have any words just yet, but he knew the sounds that dogs, cats and ducks made, and he'd make a loud quacking sound whenever he saw a bird, anything from the seagulls that frequently circled overhead to the little robin who'd taken to sitting on the outer sill of our kitchen window. I'd been trying to teach Charlie to say Mama, and he'd mastered the Ma bit and would repeat it over and over again. He was also prone to the giggles and would dissolve into helpless laughter at least ten times a day. I hadn't known it was possible to love someone so much.

It wasn't just me he got to, either; he had the same effect on everyone. Dickens might have been St Nicholas Bay's favourite Charlie for two centuries, but Christmas Past was all he had left. My Charlie was the Bay's new favourite and he had Christmas Present all sewn up.

'What sort of present would suit Uncle Will?' I chatted absently over the back of the buggy as we made our way down the high street in the second week of December. The Christmas decorations were strung up across the road, as they always had been: scenes from *A Christmas Carol* just beginning to show up more clearly against the sky, as the light faded, turning it from dark grey to black. I glanced at my watch. It was already four pm. The days just seemed to rush past. Getting out of the house with Charlie was a military operation in itself. His changing bag took more packing than a suitcase for a two-week break had back in my childless days.

'And what about Auntie Meg and Auntie Sara?' There was only an hour until the shops shut, but maybe something would hit me with inspiration. If not, there was always the Internet, but I wanted to choose my friends something personal, if I could, to thank them for their support over the past year.

As I passed the door of Cecil's Adventures, a combined café and bookshop run by Rosie from the Old St Nickers, the door flew open and the smell of mulled wine and ginger bread filled the air. It might have been one of the few places not to have its name influenced by Dickens, but everything else about

Cecil's Adventures screamed Christmas. I looked up to see who'd come hurtling out of the café in such a hurry.

'Will!'

'What a coincidence, I was just in there buying something for my favourite little boy.' Will bent down and spoke to Charlie. 'The question is, have you been good for your mummy?' Charlie just giggled in response. 'Alright, forget it, as if I could ever refuse you anything.' Will stood upright again. 'I wanted him to have this, for you to read to him on Christmas Eve.' He handed me a copy of *The Night Before Christmas*, with beautifully old-fashioned illustrations on the hard-backed cover.

'Oh, Will, it's gorgeous.' Part of me wanted to invite him to spend Christmas with us, to help me read the book to Charlie, but I daren't. I needed to get past this blip in my feelings for him first. I couldn't risk a glass or two of Champagne making me less guarded—our friendship was too important. 'So how are things at school?'

'It's not the same without you.' It was a simple statement that meant a lot. Will ran a hand through his dark hair and gave me a wry smile, as if the words had come out before he'd had a chance to stop them.

'I miss you too.' I caught myself just in time. We were both on dangerous ground. 'You, Sara, the kids, everyone.'

'But you and Charlie are going to have the best Christmas ever, and now you can send him to bed on Christmas Eve with a story from his Uncle Will.' He smiled and for a second time I longed to ask him to come and read the story to Charlie himself, tell him that if he was there *that* would make our Christmas.

I had to dig my fingernails into my palm to stop myself.

'What about you, what are your plans, now that our folks have abandoned us again for a sunshine cruise?' I kept my tone light and an unreadable expression crossed his face.

'I've had a couple of invites, one from Sara and one from an old friend back in Wales.' He shrugged. 'Sara's nagging me for a decision but I'm not sure yet. If the weather doesn't turn too nasty, I might head up to Wales.'

'Can we get together before you go?' I'd lied to Will, when we'd first talked about Christmas, told him that I'd decided it was best if it were just me and Charlie this year, so we could bond, scared he'd see the truth written all over my face every time I looked at him.

'I hope so. Bye, Charlie, bye Kate.' Will leant down towards me, his lips warm as they brushed against my cheek, before he crossed the road and disappeared into the growing darkness. Was I being an idiot not telling him how I felt? For a split second I thought about calling after him, but I needed a sense check, needed to run it past someone who would give it to me straight, provide the sensible perspective. There was only one person for the job—Meg.

Tiny Tim's Toys was like a shrine to Christmas. Outside the doors were two wooden sentry boxes that Meg's husband, James, had made. The boxes stood five feet high and housed two painted wooden soldiers, guarding the rest of the delights inside the shop. The bay windows provided the perfect showcase for the handmade toys that were the shop's speciality. There was a working carousel going around in the centre of one of the windows and, in the other, a rocking horse being ridden by two ragdolls and a teddy bear that was twice the size of Charlie.

Inside was a Christmas tree, so heavily adorned with candy canes and strings of popcorn, that the green pines beneath them were barely visible. A CD of *Rudolph the Red Nosed Reindeer* was playing in the background and the shop was bustling. James was serving and, for a moment, I thought Meg wasn't there. Then I spotted her, in the corner of the shop, deep in conversation with Sara.

Even better, I could tell them both at the same time. I knew I could trust them with my feelings for Will and they'd know more than anyone if it was good idea for me to tell him or not.

Meg finally looked in my direction and waved, although she didn't smile. Sara was looking uncharacteristically serious too.

'How's my favourite boy?' Sara echoed Will's words from earlier and had scooped Charlie out of the buggy and on to her hip before I could even respond. Thank goodness he'd bonded with me as well as he had; Sara definitely didn't have the knack of holding back. It was lovely to see, though, and I wondered whether she would have wanted more children, given the chance. It was the one thing she never really spoke about. Still, she'd got her application into university at the beginning of December, acted on the thing she said she'd have liked to ask Miss Bone—it seemed we were all finding our way after almost a year without our old teacher.

'He's great, we both are.' I pulled the buggy to one side, as an overly-enthusiastic little boy ducked under my arm towards a display of wooden animals. 'I'm really glad you're both here, actually. I wanted to talk to you about something.' I looked around the busy shop, and thankfully Meg read my mind.

'Not here, eh?' She called across to James. 'I'm just going up to the flat with the girls.'

Folding the buggy with newfound expertise, I followed the two of them up the stairs, Charlie still sitting happily on Sara's hip.

'Where's Riley?' Looking around the flat, I had to smile. Clearly her son was as well trained as you'd expect with a mother like Meg. There was no Lego strewn across the floor to form an obstacle course for any passing adult and her tree had decorations hanging from even the lowest branches.

'It's so busy at the moment, Mum's been having him after playgroup, giving him his tea and then bringing him home.' Meg gave a wry smile. 'It's kind of ironic when you're so busy running a toy shop that you don't get to see your own child. It won't last long, though. It's just a December thing and we can't afford not to do it when we make half our yearly profits this month alone.'

'God, I should have thought. Look if you need to get back to help James out, we can talk some other time.'

'No way! I've earned twenty minutes off and there are three cups of cinnamon coffee with our names on. In fact, Sara and I were going to head up for a cup just before you arrived. I'll take some down to James when we've finished and he can take a break for a bit then.' Meg busied herself making the drinks, as I passed Sara a rusk to keep Charlie busy and away from the gingerbread men stacked in a bowl on Meg's coffee table.

'How does she keep Riley away from all this stuff? Charlie's in to everything. He ate half of one of my lipsticks yesterday, but if you happen to bump into my social worker, I'd rather you didn't mention it.'

'What type was it?' Sara put the rusk in Charlie's outstretched hand.

'Chanel, I think, why?'

'Just checking, and he's got impeccable taste at least.' Sara smiled, but I wasn't convinced. She definitely wasn't her usual happy-go-lucky self.

'Here you go, my lovelies.' Meg brought over a tray of frothy cinnamon coffees and put them at the furthest end of the table, well away from Charlie. 'What's this burning news then, Kate?'

'It's about Will, there's something I need to tell you.' I paused, and Sara clamped a hand to her chest.

'Oh, thank God, he's told you.' She smiled and for the first time it reached her eyes. 'I thought I was going to have to break it to you.'

'Sorry, what?' I shook my head, confused, she couldn't possibly know what I was going to say. 'I think we're talking at cross purposes.'

'You don't know about Will leaving the school? He handed his notice in last week and he leaves at the spring half-term holiday in February.' She put her coffee down with a thud and some of it spilled on to the table top. I vaguely registered that things must be serious, since Meg hadn't vaulted over the back of the sofa to get a cloth to wipe it up.

'He's leaving. Why?' It was as though all the air had been knocked out of my lungs.

'We don't really know. I'm guessing it's a job elsewhere and he's been going backwards and forwards to Wales since the summer.' Meg looked at me levelly. 'We actually thought you might be the one in the know.'

'He hasn't mentioned it to me. *At all.*' I was still struggling to get the words out.

'I'm sure he will next time he sees you.' Sara looked almost as miserable as I felt. 'I guess he just didn't want to tell you over the phone.'

'I saw him ten minutes ago, outside Cecil's Adventures. He didn't say a word.' I pushed the coffee away, trying desperately to think straight. He couldn't be going back to Wales, back to Louisa, could he?

'It'll be so weird him not being around. It's been so great to have all the old gang back together again for these last few years and, try as I might, I never liked Louisa any more than she liked us.' Meg snapped the head off a gingerbread man, and I wished I could do the same to Louisa. She couldn't have Will, she didn't deserve him. He should be with someone like... Well, someone who was anyone but Louisa.

'So if you weren't going to tell us about Will's new job, what *did* you want to say?' Sara was also snapping the limbs off a gingerbread man and absently dunking them into her coffee. Meg still hadn't told her off for the mess she was making.

'I just wanted some advice about what to get him for Christmas.' It sounded lame, but no-one questioned me further. We were all too shocked about Will leaving the Bay, and suddenly the idea of Christmas had lost its shine.

Chapter Fourteen

I only saw Will once more, when the four of us got together for a pre-Christmas meal at Sara's house. Maybe he was trying to avoid me, deliberately; I don't know. Either way, I didn't get a chance to speak to him on our own and he skirted around the issue when he replied to my texts. Yes, he'd been offered a job, it involved a lot of travelling–so he wasn't sure yet where he'd be based and was getting his cottage valued just in case—but he didn't reveal any of the details. It didn't sound like he was taking a headship in Wales, which was what I was most of afraid of—because Wales meant Louisa—but he wasn't confiding in me and I realised, with a heavy heart, that something had irrevocably changed between us. I wished I'd told him how I felt earlier. If he was leaving, anyway, it obviously wouldn't have changed things, but now it seemed stupid not to have done it and the moment had passed.

Christmas Eve arrived with a light scattering of snow, and I smiled at the text from Mum, sent when they'd stopped off in Mexico on their cruise:

✉ from: Mum
It's 80 degrees here today, Dad says he'll be forced to go sock-less if it gets any hotter! Happy Christmas Eve, darling girl and Charlie-boy, love you both to the moon and back and we'll ring you tomorrow xxxx

Mum never abbreviated anything in her messages and she was the only person I knew who was inclined to include a semi-colon or circumflex in her texts, if the need arose.

'I think we might need two pairs of socks, unlike Nanny and Grandad.' I pulled the snowsuit onto Charlie's legs and eased it up past his shoulders. He was being quite compliant, which was good. A walk around the harbour on a frosty evening like this definitely required several layers.

Charlie grinned at me as I zipped him up. I was so blessed, it was greedy to ask for anything else for Christmas, but part of me was hoping we might bump into Will and get a chance to talk. Really talk.

Strapping Charlie into his buggy, I tucked a couple of extra blankets around his knees and put on my scarf and hat. St Nicholas, being the patron saint of sailors, was the real origin of the town's name, which had been hijacked by Christmas over the years. It made the location of the tiny chapel, right on the edge of the harbour, a natural choice. Every Christmas Eve, the St Nicholas Bay choir would meet outside to sing carols and even the odd sea shanty.

The chapel was far too tiny for a full-blown service, so I was glad we were both bundled up in extra layers as I got closer to the harbour and a vicious north wind blew off the sea, whipping at the ends of my scarf. There wasn't enough snow to cause any real problem and it had frosted to a hard crust which crunched beneath my feet and the wheels of Charlie's buggy.

There were rows of moored boats bobbing up and down on the water, most of them strung with Christmas lights. Cratchit's oyster house, which people travelled from miles around to visit, on the opposite side of the u-shaped harbour, reverberated with laughter and music. I'd passed Nachos At The Bay on the way down, too, and through the windows I could see that every table had been full. The restaurants and pubs in St Nicholas Bay were always really busy on Christmas Eve, but it had been a family tradition of ours to head down and listen to the choir in the early evening and it was something I wanted to continue now that I had a family of my own. Sara's children had long since grown out of it, but Meg would be there with Riley, and I was looking forward to seeing a friendly face.

Sara had told us that Will had turned down the invitation for Christmas lunch at her house, which meant he was going to Wales for Christmas and, despite hoping he'd be at the harbour, I knew he was probably already half way up the M4.

Light was visible through the stained-glass windows of the chapel as I rounded the corner and I could hear the choir, even over the sound of an entirely different type of singing coming from the oyster house.

Meg was already in position and she waved enthusiastically as I pushed Charlie's buggy towards her, stopping briefly to lean down and check he was warm enough, tucking his blankets more securely around his legs. Charlie grabbed hold of my necklace as I did so and grated his teeth across the wooden beads before I untangled us both.

There was a large Christmas tree hung with gold stars on one side of the chapel. They were from the memorial service held on the first Sunday of Advent where friends and family gathered at the harbourside to remember loved ones missing at Christmas, as well as sailors lost at sea in years gone by. You could write a message to anyone no longer with you on the back of one of the gold stars and hang it on the tree. Sara, Meg and I had all been to the service and hung up a star for Miss Bone, and Meg had hung one for her father too, as she always did, who'd died in a boating accident two months before she was born. Will had been away for the weekend of the memorial service as well, probably with Louisa. I tried not to think evil thoughts—standing outside a chapel on Christmas Eve really wasn't the place for those.

The choir stood directly in front of the chapel doors and a small group of children from St Nicolas Bay primary were singing some of the carols with them. A couple of them noticed me and waved, one even called out to me. I held my finger up to my lips, urging them to concentrate on the task in hand, I knew how short the average six-year-old's attention span could be. The children were dressed as angels and someone had even sourced halos that lit up in the darkness. I was impressed at their parents inventiveness and suppressed a smile, knowing I had all this to come with Charlie.

I held it together through the children's renditions of *Little Donkey* and *Away in Manager*. Then the choir sang *Love Came Down at Christmas* and I couldn't help thinking of Will, wondering whether it was love that was driving him out of the Bay. When the choir sang *O Holy Night*, which had always been my favourite, I remembered how much Miss Bone had loved it too. I felt choked with emotion, happy and heartbroken all at the same time. The prospect of Will going back to Louisa hurt like hell and, even if he hadn't turned out to be Botoxed-up to the eyebrows, literally, and completely insensitive to boot, that eighteen-year-long crush I'd had on Simon Miller had been less than nothing in comparison.

'Kate, are you okay?' Meg's hand was over mine. 'The atmosphere always gets to me too.' I nodded. I didn't want to tell Sara and Meg how I felt about Will any more. It was my secret, my issue to get over, and their sympathy would just make things worse.

'Happy Christmas, Meg.' I gave her a hug after the choir finished their final song, turning down her offer of a Christmas drink back at their place, and thanked the foresight of having exchanged presents earlier in the week; I couldn't bear the thought of struggling back up the frosty pavements, pushing Charlie and a big stack of gifts. Just as I'd predicted, my family and friends had spoilt him rotten and there were too many presents for him to fit under the tree. I tried not to think about the fact that Will hadn't left either of us a present. After all, he'd bought that lovely book and it was silly to expect anything else. I didn't want anything from him but his company anyway.

Walking up the hill towards the flat, we passed the scene strung across the road in lights depicting the Ghost of Christmas Yet to Come. For once, I didn't get that familiar sense of foreboding as I went underneath and Charlie giggled at something that had taken his fancy. Maybe, with a wonderful little boy in my life, I'd finally outgrown the fear of a spectre from the future.

Inside the flat was warm and I took out my DVD of *The Muppet Christmas Carol*. Like most St Nicholas Bay locals, I had almost every version of the film ever made, but this seemed most apt for my first Christmas as a mum. And who didn't love the Muppets? I warmed some milk for my son and made myself an indulgent hot chocolate with whipped cream and marshmallows. Charlie helped me hang our stockings either side of the ornamental fireplace, the chimney of which had been blocked years earlier, before we settled down together. I don't know if he had any idea what was going on, but I was locking every moment in the memory box inside my head. The magic of Christmas was back for the first time since I'd stopped being a believer in *you know who*. It would be a year or two before we could leave out mince pies for Father Christmas and carrots for the reindeer, but I couldn't wait.

Charlie snuggled into the crook of my arm as we lay on the sofa and was asleep long before the Ghost of Christmas Yet to Come made his appearance. He stirred when I carried him to bed and so I read *The Night Before Christmas* to him, watching his eyelids get heavier and heavier as I pointed out the pictures.

Once he was asleep, I idly flicked through the channels on TV, stretching out along the sofa, before settling on Christmas 24 and a continuous feed of feel-good seasonal films, almost all about love arriving more or less in tandem with Santa Claus himself.

I was lucky not to have to fight anyone for control of the remote, or have to watch the *Top Gear* Christmas Special, and to be able to lie full length on the sofa. Maybe we'd find someone like Will to share our lives eventually, but I already had the Christmas I'd always wanted.

Chapter Fifteen

It's funny the things tradition makes you do. There I was, cooking Christmas dinner for one adult and an almost-two-year-old child, and we had a turkey that probably weighed more than Charlie.

My gorgeous little man had enjoyed unwrapping his presents, but after it was all over, he was far more interested in the gift-wrap and was sitting in one of the boxes his toys had come in, banging the side of it with a plastic hammer. I was just basting the turkey for about the millionth time and was wrestling to turn it over—so the juices would keep the meat moist, as Jamie Oliver had promised—when someone rang the doorbell. I had a Christmas CD playing in the lounge, which had launched into a rendition of *Frosty the Snowman*, but the persistent ringing of the doorbell easily drowned it out.

'Hang on.' I shoved the turkey back into the oven, wrong side up, and scooped Charlie up from the living room floor on the way past; he was still waving his plastic hammer in the air. 'I swear to God, darling, if this turns out to be Jehovah's Witnesses, you're about to be a witness yourself to your mum throttling someone.'

'Ho, ho, ho!' As I opened the door, Father Christmas filled the frame. He had a well-padded stomach, but the face behind the white beard looked far too young to pass for Santa Claus. 'I hear there's a little boy in this house who's very definitely on my good list.' The attempt to deepen the tone couldn't disguise the voice I'd known so well for thirty years, and I moved instantly to let Will step inside.

Charlie's eyes widened at the sight of a strange man in a red and white suit dominating the space and his bottom lip started to wobble.

'I think you might need to show him it's you.' As I spoke, Will whipped off the hat and beard and followed us through to the lounge.

'Hey, buddy, it's just your Uncle Will.' Charlie looked at him for a moment and then started giggling. 'God, I'm sorry, I didn't think this through. I hope I haven't put him off Santa Claus for life.'

'I don't think he's too traumatised.' Charlie squirmed in my arms, eager to get back to his cardboard box boat, or whatever it was, so I put him down on the floor.

'I thought you were going away for Christmas.' I tried to keep my tone casual, but I couldn't help noticing the violet shadows under Will's eyes, and I longed to reach out and smooth down the hair that was now sticking up as a result of being shoved into a Santa hat.

'I'm sorry, I know this was supposed to be your Christmas with just Charlie and I tried to stay away, I really did, but I just couldn't do it.' Will lowered his eyes and I desperately tried not to read too much into his words.

'But you're leaving. Going back to Wales?' As I said the words, he looked up at me and somehow I knew I'd got it all wrong. 'We all thought you were going back to Louisa, to try again.'

'God no! The only reason I've been going up to Wales is to sort out stuff with the house and Louisa once and for all. I needed to leave the job at school because I wanted to take a chance on saying something to you that might mean we couldn't work together any more—either because it was against the rules to be in a relationship, or because I'd be too embarrassed to ever look you in the eyes again. It was why I got the cottage valued too. I'm not as tied to the Bay with my new job. I kept hold of your presents, so I'd have an excuse to come and see you and Charlie.' Will's green eyes met mine for a moment and I had to hold back from launching myself into his arms. 'And to bring you this.' He passed me a small album, the sort with photos you slot into individual plastic sleeves.

'Oh my God, they're all of the school trip to Paris. I had no idea you had so many.' I laughed as I flicked through it. It seemed so dated looking back, and we'd thought those plaid blazers would never go out of fashion. 'Where did you dig it out from?'

'I didn't.' It was hot in the lounge and he was dressed as Father Christmas, but I wasn't sure if the colour in his cheeks could be entirely put down to that. 'I've always known where it was, and I've looked at the photo of you on the top of the Eiffel Tower hundreds of times. It was just before, you know…'

'We kissed?' As his eyes met mine, I realised the risk of telling him how I felt wasn't a risk any more.

'I wish I'd had the balls to tell you back then how I felt, but you didn't seem like you wanted me to.' He tried for a casual shrug, but it didn't quite come off.

'And there I was, thinking the same.' The words had slipped out of my mouth before I could stop them. Knowing that Will felt the same—then and now—had steamrollered my defences.

'For years I was kicking myself, for missing my chance, but if I don't tell you now, I never will.'

'Go on, I'm listening.' I was still too chicken to tell him the truth, so I was going to have to let him say what needed to be said.

'Do you remember when Sara asked us what question we wished we'd had the chance to ask Miss Bone, in the pub after the funeral, and I said I wanted to know if I was always going to be on my own? You said half the women at the school were in love with me and I mumbled something you didn't hear because I didn't have the guts to say it out loud?' Will paused and I nodded. 'What I said was that half the women might be in love with me, but not the one I want. You were the only person I ever wanted to tell me that, for as long as I can remember, probably from when we weren't much older than Charlie. But you only ever wanted to be my friend. Being your friend was better than being nothing at all, so I forced myself to accept that it would never happen. I think I chose Louisa because she was so different to you. I didn't want someone who reminded me of you, but would only ever be a poor imitation, when I wanted the real thing. So I went for the polar opposite.'

'I thought you'd fallen madly in love with her, and I hated her on sight.' I had to sit down, it was so much to take in. Will sat down next to me.

'I didn't want to push you, but a few times since Miss Bone died I felt like there was a chance you might see me as more than just a friend, but it was still a huge risk to ask you that outright. I knew you wouldn't do anything to jeopardise the adoption anyway and I didn't want to either. I had every intention of waiting until I start my new job in

February, and by then Charlie will have been with you for over ten weeks and you can lodge the adoption with the court. But I couldn't stop myself coming to see you both today. Christmas, or any day, isn't the same without you. I had to take the chance and tell you, because it's killing me either way.'

'Will…' I was leaving him hanging, but I couldn't find the words. When you'd been holding back your feelings for half a lifetime, it was hard to just let go.

'If you don't say something,' he managed a half-smile, 'then I'll have no alternative but to start singing and I won't stop until you tell me how you feel.' He opened his mouth, as though he was about to start, and I laughed—the tension broken.

'You're right, I stopped seeing you as just a friend a while back, but I was terrified of losing that friendship at the same time. I've been wanting to tell you how I felt, for weeks, ever since Halloween.' I blushed at the memory but, now I'd started, the floodgates had opened and my feelings were spilling out, whether I wanted them to or not. 'It was like a light bulb switched on in my head that night. Only I told myself it would never happen, that eventually Charlie and I would find someone *like* you to complete our family. Only there isn't anyone like you. Not for me.'

For a moment Will's face flooded with relief, but then he took my hand, a serious expression replacing the smile that had been there only seconds before. 'You've got no idea how much it means to me to hear that, but there's one more thing I need to tell you before you decide if you really want to be with me.

I've got a horrible feeling it might change everything.'

I swallowed, trying desperately to work out what it was, as the worst possible scenarios flashed through my mind: maybe Louisa was pregnant, the result of one last night together, or Will had some terrible illness. 'Go on.'

'It's my new job. I'm not sure how to put this, I'm a… school inspector.'

'Will Thomas, how could you!' I was already laughing as he pulled me towards him. 'As it's you, I think I might just be able to look past it.'

'Are you sure? What about the ban on new relationships?' The look on Will's face made it obvious the last thing he wanted was to stay away for another six weeks.

'There's nothing new about this.' I put my hand over his. 'It's already turning into the best Christmas I've ever had and I've got a feeling we've got years of them yet to come.'

'That's all I've ever wanted.' Finally he kissed me and Charlie pealed into giggles, as the CD moved on a track and *I Saw Mommy Kissing Santa Claus* started up.

'You're wearing red and white.' I pulled away from Will, with the sudden realisation, and looked at my son in his red pyjamas covered in white snowflakes. My family was complete, in red and white, just as Cyril had predicted. Although, unless I was very much mistaken, someone else had definitely had a hand in things—I could feel it in my bones.

The End

Other Work by Jo Bartlett

Winter Tales

Jo is a featured author in The Write Romantics charity anthology 'Winter Tales' available via Amazon in paperback and e-book formats.

As the days become chilly and the evenings draw in, why not cosy up with us this winter and enjoy our anthology of stories to warm the heart? The Write Romantics present their first anthology of uplifting short stories by skilled and published writers, created just for you. So light the fire, settle down on the sofa, and prepare to spend Christmas in July, meet The Handsome Stranger, or fall in love with Mr Perfect. Just a taste of our twenty-four stories to bring a smile to your lips and touch your soul, knowing that all proceeds of this anthology will go to The Cystic Fibrosis Trust and the Teenage Cancer Trust.

Among a Thousand Stars

Jo's first full-length novel will be available from So Vain Books in June 2015 in paperback and e-book formats at www.sovainbooks.co.uk.

*When her mother turns up naked and proud during her first term at college, Ashleigh Hayes assumes that life can't get any more embarrassing. Ten years later, with best friend Stevie at her side, and a successful career as a freelance photographer for monthly magazine **Glitz**, it looks like she might have finally got the hang of things. Only she seems to have inherited the embarrassment gene from her mother* *and her every encounter with new boss, Tom Rushworth, looks set to send her career spiraling backwards. Getting past their shaky start, Ashleigh and Tom embark on a relationship that was only ever meant to be a bit of fun. But when life, paparazzi and love-sick Labradors get in the way, they suddenly find themselves caught up on a roller coaster ride neither of them can control.*

Printed in Great Britain
by Amazon.co.uk, Ltd.,
Marston Gate.